FaR~
Fetched

Also by Lisa Papademetriou

Hearts & Crafts series

Squad Goals

Pet Project

Confectionately Yours series

Save the Cupcake!

Taking the Cake!

Sugar and Spice

Something New

Accidentally series

Accidentally Fabulous

Accidentally Famous

Accidentally Fooled

Accidentally Friends

A Tale of Highly Unusual Magic

Apartment 1986

The Dreamway

Ice Dreams

How to Be a Girly Girl in Just Ten Days

Far-Fetched

BY LISA PAPADEMETRIOU

SCHOLASTIC INC.

Text copyright © 2025 by Lisa Papademetriou

All rights reserved. Published by Scholastic Inc., *Publishers since 1920*. SCHOLASTIC and associated logos are trademarks and/or registered trademarks of Scholastic Inc.

The publisher does not have any control over and does not assume any responsibility for author or third-party websites or their content.

No part of this publication may be reproduced, stored in a retrieval system, or transmitted in any form or by any means, electronic, mechanical, photocopying, recording, or otherwise, or used to train any artificial intelligence technologies, without written permission of the publisher. For information regarding permission, write to Scholastic Inc., Attention: Permissions Department, 557 Broadway, New York, NY 10012.

This book is a work of fiction. Names, characters, places, and incidents are either the product of the author's imagination or are used fictitiously, and any resemblance to actual persons, living or dead, business establishments, events, or locales is entirely coincidental.

ISBN 978-1-338-60308-8

10 9 8 7 6 5 4 3 2 1   25 26 27 28 29

Printed in the U.S.A.   40

First printing 2025

Book design by Maithili Joshi

For Willa Barman

CHAPTER ONE

Coimetrophobia—fear of cemeteries

Are people just afraid of cemeteries, or are they actually afraid of ghosts? I'm not sure if I even believe in ghosts. I think I don't, but then I feel kind of bad about it—like, what if the ghosts are out there, and they're super-bummed that people don't believe in them? Maybe if I did believe in them, they'd feel better about themselves and rest in peace. But I suppose I'm not *afraid* of ghosts. I'm just afraid that I might be letting them down without knowing it.

Either way...it's kind of a bummer to think that even people who are afraid of cemeteries will probably end up in one.

"Phones away, please!" Monique said in her best imitation of our social studies teacher as she plopped onto the low stone wall beside me and swept her long black braids over her shoulder.

"Dead-on Dobbler voice, Mo," Harry said, giving her a high five. With a bright smile, he leaned against the trunk of the old oak tree whose branches grew over the wall, extending beyond the graveyard. Then he lifted his straight black eyebrows at my phone.

"Just a minute," I said, typing faster. As usual, my two best friends were ten minutes late for our walk, so I'd done what everyone does while they're waiting—gotten engrossed in my phone.

Harry reached into his pocket for his own phone, and Monique warned, "Don't even think about it. I didn't come here to hang out with people shooting digital zombies."

Harry held up his hands in mock surrender. "I was just going to look up a recipe for Chex mix."

I'm usually the one complaining about my friends being on their phones—Harry, in particular, loves to play games while he's talking to us. It irritates Monique beyond words. So far beyond words, in fact, that she started snapping her fingers at me in a general hurry-up way.

"One sec, one sec!"

Monique crossed her arms over her chest. "Who are you texting?"

"No one," I said. "I'm filling out the form to run for class secretary."

"You're actually going to run?" Monique looked shocked. "Seriously?" She leaned over to look at my screen.

I sighed. "Well . . . I'm thinking about it."

"Wow." Harry pursed his lips and lifted his eyebrows into an I'm-impressed expression. "That seems like a stretch for your comfort zone."

"My parents are insisting that I do an activity next year,"

I explained. "Linden is doing about fifty extracurriculars now, and my dad keeps hinting around that I'd have all of those opportunities, too, *if I went to a private school.*"

Harry and Monique exchanged a nervous glance, and Harry asked, "You think they'd send you to Greenwood?"

"Not if I'm a class officer at *our* school," I told them.

It was still twilight, and the sky was purply gray, with only a few scattered pale stars. A lonely cricket was chirping his heart out, and the old graves—some very thin and faded with age—sat like crooked dark arches in the cemetery beyond. It sounds creepy, I guess, but the cemetery is actually beautiful, like a park. There are walking paths and lots of trees and even a few large crypts—miniature green hobbit hills with doors in them—that have been around for hundreds of years. It seems too old for anything terrible to happen there. Like, the ghosts of three centuries ago were probably too refined to bother haunting a bunch of seventh graders like us.

"But I'm still not one hundred percent sure I should run," I said, turning back to my friends.

"The deadline is in three hours and twenty minutes," Harry pointed out.

"Thank you, Harry, I know."

"So what's the holdup?" Monique gestured for me to hand her my phone.

I scrolled to the top of the Google form and passed it to her. "You have to write a three-sentence description of why you want the job and why you'd be good at it. That goes on the ballot."

"This is five sentences." Monique frowned.

Harry sat down beside her and leaned in to read the form. "Maybe use a semicolon?"

"Does a semicolon look pretentious?" I asked.

"We are not writing a biography of Abraham Lincoln, Harry," Monique said. "No semicolons. Lizzie, you can just delete the first sentence where you say your name and grade and stuff—that information is going to be on the ballot, anyway. And you can get rid of the last one, too."

"I just wanted to remind people what being class secretary is all about," I said.

"Yes, but I think people already know that the class secretary is in charge of planning fundraisers. I mean, everyone is looking forward to the eighth-grade trip. And if the class government doesn't raise the funds, it's going to be terrible."

Harry nodded. "They're thinking of canceling."

"What?" Monique demanded, still editing my application. "Where did you hear that?"

"I told him," I said. "I heard it at the school committee meeting." Yes, once a month I like to curl up with a bowl of Cheetos and watch an administrative meeting on Zoom. It's kind of my *thang*. Okay, yeah, I just realized how nerdy that probably sounds, but trust me, it's *actually* very . . . well, okay, I guess it *is* nerdy.

"I can't believe you watch those meetings." Shaking her head, Monique tapped the screen, then handed the phone back to me, announcing, "Less is more."

I read the shorter sentences, and she was right—it was better. "But do you think it sounds conceited to say that I'm organized?"

Monique looked at Harry, who shrugged and said, "It sounds *accurate*. I mean, your closet is organized by color."

"Everyone does that," I said.

"No offense, but it's becoming very clear that I'm your only guy friend."

"That's not a girl thing, Harry," Monique shot back. "Nobody else does that. Lizzie, you literally made your own class directory last year when the school didn't put one out." Monique pushed herself off the stone wall, and I followed. "You're the reason everyone in the class can text each other." We headed through the open black iron gate and up the wide main path of the graveyard, toward the Civil War monument honoring our town's Union soldiers.

"Well, that was just ridiculous," I said. Damp leaves covered the gravel path and stuck to the bottom of my shoes as we walked. "When people are sick, how are they supposed to get the homework? Or figure out how to get together for group projects?"

"It isn't conceited to say something factual," Harry said.

"It's not like you're saying that you're gorgeous, which would be an opinion," Monique added.

Harry nodded. "And would reveal bias." Our social studies teacher, Ms. Dobbler, has been teaching us to "evaluate the quality of our sources" so that we're not just presenting some random I-Did-My-Own-Research guy's YouTube video as evidence that the world is actually a cube run by lizard people.

Side note—my friends actually *are* gorgeous. We've been friends so long that I don't usually notice, but they both look like lifestyle influencers, while I, with my straight brown hair and functional wardrobe, look more like the kind of person who gets influenced. Monique's parents are from Haiti, and she has huge wide-set eyes with long lashes and skin that's sleek and brown like polished wood. Harry is part English, part Danish, part Japanese, and part Jamaican, and he has dark eyebrows over hazel eyes, curly blond hair, and skin the color of sand. And I'm a Greek-Scottish white girl with braces, stubby eyelashes, and a wardrobe of solid color T-shirts that I wear with basic blue jeans.

Harry poked me in the arm and nodded at my phone. "Send it," he urged.

I grimaced. "I don't know. I'm still not sure I'm going to do it. I was just going to see how I was feeling around the deadline, you know?"

"Why?" Harry asked.

"Just go for it," Monique put in.

"I just . . . ugh. What if I lose?"

"Is anyone else running?" Harry asked. "Aren't your odds of winning a hundred percent?"

"It doesn't matter!" Monique stopped walking. "I'll be your campaign manager. If someone else runs, I will make sure that you crush them." I hesitated, and Monique added, "Do not chicken out of this, Lizzie. You'll be great at it."

I looked over the application again. "I don't know," I said. "Does this description sound okay? Should I get rid of this exclamation point?"

"Let me see," Monique said. I gave her the phone, and she touched the screen. "Oops," she said. With a mischievous smile, she handed it back.

Your form has been submitted!

A moment passed before my hand went cold and my stomach dropped. "What did you do?" My voice was a whisper. An all-too-familiar nausea worked its way up my throat.

"I started managing your campaign."

Harry nodded at Monique with this impressed look on his face. "I want you to know that I would really like to high-five you right now, but I'm afraid that Lizzie will throttle me," he said. "So instead, I'm going to do this victory dance."

Monique and Harry did a little groove as I stood there, sweating and staring at my phone. Finally, they noticed that I was actually frozen.

"I'm sorry, Lizzie," Monique said, standing still again. "Are you really mad?"

Yes! Yes, I was. And I had that tight-throat feeling and my stomach was queasy.

Right on cue, an image popped into my mind: *The principal calls me onstage to announce that I've lost the election.*

I look out at the audience—everyone in my grade is there, and everyone is booing. Someone throws a head of lettuce at me and I duck, accidentally knocking Principal Yeoh into the orchestra pit . . .

"Hey." Monique placed a hand gently on my arm. "Are you imagining the worst-case scenario right now?" She knows the way my mind works.

I nodded and told them what my imagination had just conjured.

"Where did the lettuce come from?" Harry asked.

"I guess someone brought it with them," I said.

"Who would do that?" Monique asked. "And *why?*"

"This is not your best worst-case scenario," Harry put in. "I'm sorry, but it's really far-fetched."

The nausea lifted and I managed to take a breath. "Because our school doesn't have an orchestra pit?"

"All of it." Harry shook his head. "Sorry."

Monique was still staring at me, clearly worried. "I'm sorry, too. Don't be mad."

"I'm not . . ." I managed to squeak.

"Oh, that's her squeaky lie voice!" Harry said, pointing at me. "Monique, that's her squeaky lie voice."

"I am well aware, Harry. Lizzie, don't worry. I'm sure that we can undo the application."

I inhaled, long and noisily. Then I exhaled.

"That's good." Harry nodded encouragingly. "Deep breathing like we learned from Dr. Funk." Our school therapist, Dr. Funk (yes, that's her real name, although she is disappointingly not funky at all) taught us how to breathe through moments that made us feel anxious.

Two more breaths and the queasiness was gone. After another, I was able to look at Monique. "Honestly, maybe it's good that you did it for me."

"Because you chicken out of things a lot?" Harry asked.

"Harry!"

"That had a question mark at the end!" Harry insisted. "It was a *question*."

I sighed. "It's okay."

"I really didn't mean to freak you out," Monique said.

"Forcing people to do things I think they'd be good at is my love language."

"I know. I feel very loved."

"You are!" Monique squeezed me in one of her typical bear hugs.

Just then, someone sneezed. We froze, staring at one another, suddenly noticing how dark it had gotten in the cemetery and how alone we were. Or how alone we *thought* we were.

"Holy . . ." I grabbed Monique's hand.

"It's not anyone undead," she said, but she didn't sound, like, *positive*.

"Hello?" Harry called.

"Sorry!" someone shouted. The voice came from the aboveground crypt at the edge of the cemetery. And then a dark figure on top of the crypt sat up quickly, and I screamed, which made Monique scream. The figure on the crypt sneezed again.

Harry laughed. "Guys, relax. It's Ant!"

The dark figure, which I could now see was a fully alive

human the same age as us, scrambled down from the crypt, and I saw that Harry was right—it was Antonio Gutierrez. Also known as: the reason Dobbler gave us extra homework last week. (She got mad because he was listening to a soccer game during class. It would have been fine if he hadn't shouted, "Goal!" while we were supposed to be finishing the exercises at the end of the chapter.)

"Hi, sorry." Ant flashed a smile. "I heard you guys talking, but I figured I'd just let you walk by because I didn't want to scare you. But then"—he shrugged—"allergies. I'm sorry I freaked you out."

Laughing, Monique jammed her hands into the front pockets of her jeans. "I nearly started running when I heard that!"

"How's it going, man?" Ant held out a fist, which Harry delightedly bumped. "It's great that you're running for secretary," Ant added with a smile, which was weird because I didn't even think he knew who I was. "I hear our grade is behind on fundraising." He raked a hand through his hair. The white gap in his left eyebrow flashed, then disappeared again behind his long bangs.

I felt Monique elbow me, and I could practically read her mind. Ant is pretty popular—he's one of those guys who gets along with everyone and is on the soccer team and gets decent grades and stuff. But he's also kind of an idiot. He literally blew part of his own eyebrow off with a firework two years ago, so I try to stay away from him. But every vote counts, right? "Well," I said, "I think I'm the only person running."

Monique elbowed me again, and even though I wasn't looking at her, I could sense that her eyes were rolling around in her head like a couple of marbles. "As Lizzie's campaign manager, I'd like to say thanks for your support."

We stood there awkwardly for a moment.

"Have you guys started studying for the social studies test yet?" Ant asked.

"Yes," I said, just as Harry asked, "What test?"

"The unit test." Monique sounded exasperated. "It's like ten percent of our grade."

"Oh, right." Harry nodded. "Friday."

"Tomorrow," I corrected.

Harry looked horrified, and I added, "Time to get started, Harry."

"I'd better get going on that, too," Ant said, backing toward the footpath. "I'll see you at school!"

"See you," I called, but he had already turned away.

My friends and I stood and watched him hurry out of the graveyard.

"That was weird," Monique said, and the moment the words were out of her mouth, I realized that we had never asked Ant what he was doing alone in a graveyard on a school night.

We walked the three blocks back to a cul-de-sac and watched as Monique continued to the end, waved, and went inside her house. Then Harry and I walked the extra block to our houses, which are next to each other. I checked my watch. "Five minutes early."

He blinked up at the sky, which was turning into a deeper gray and sprinkled with faint stars. "It's still a little bit light out."

"I love it when the days are finally long enough to stay out until after seven," I said. In the part of Massachusetts where we live, winter is cold and really dark. In December, it's pitch-black at 4:00 p.m. Now that it's April, the sun is finally coming back.

Harry waved and jogged up his front walk.

My grandmother's car was in our driveway, so I took a deep breath before I opened the side door. She lives in the town next to ours—about six miles away—which is far enough for her to complain that we never come to see her, but close enough for her to "drop by" to see us more or less constantly.

I walked inside to find her sitting at the dining table, drinking a mug of tea with pursed lips. "Well, well, well, where have you been?"

"Out walking with my friends," I said. "Hi, Mimi." I came over and gave her a little hug around the shoulders, which she sort of leaned into. She's not really a hugger. I think she doesn't like to rumple her clothes. As she likes to point out, *They're expensive, dear.*

"She's allowed to hang out with her friends until seven forty-five," Mom explained, pulling the tea towel from her shoulder and tucking it into the fridge handle. My mom is kind of the opposite of my grandmother—always somewhat rumpled.

"Even in the dark?" Mimi asked. "Is that safe?"

"She's with her friends," Mom said.

"And I have my phone," I added. "In case I have a problem."

"What do you say about it, Gerald?" Mimi called to my dad, who was on the couch with his computer in his lap. He was frowning at the screen, typing away.

Mom's eyes expanded in a sort of I'm-going-to-lose-it expression, which—of course—my grandmother didn't notice because she had kept her back to the kitchen during the entire conversation.

Dad kept typing.

"Dad!"

He looked up. "Hm?"

"Mimi wants to know if it's okay for me to walk around outside when it's dark."

Dad looked from me to his mother, who tilted her head expectantly. Then he looked back at me. "Sure," he said. "Have fun."

I rolled my eyes. That was *so* Dad. He gets super-focused when he's working. "No, Dad, I'm back already."

"Gerald," Mimi went on insistently, "don't you think it's dangerous for a young girl to be walking around alone at night?" Frowning, she straightened the sad mums in the chipped pitcher on the table.

Dad peered at the clock on the mantel. "Mom, it's not even seven forty."

"Still, it's not as if she's walking around the campus at Greenwood, where there are security guards. Something might *happen*."

Dad cocked his head, like he was thinking this over, but my mom jumped in.

"Emilia, we know all the neighbors. Besides, Lizzie's with Monique and Harry, and they all have phones. This town hasn't changed much since Gerald was Lizzie's age."

"And you used to let me and Dave walk around after dinner all the time," Dad added.

I don't know if it's possible to drink tea "disapprovingly," but if it *is* possible, then Mimi did it. Finally, she placed the mug down carefully, pushed back her chair, and stood up. "I see," she said. That's what she says when she doesn't approve of something. I know it bugs my mom, but Dad just went back to typing. "Well, Francine, I think I'll be heading home. If I could just get that platter?"

"Oh, right." Mom opened the cabinet and moved a few dishes to get to the fancy silver platter. She swiped at a bit of dust on the edge, then handed it over to my grandmother.

"Oh, is that where you usually keep it?" Mimi asked, as if we had some extra, secret hidden cupboards in another section of our tiny house. My grandmother gave my parents the platter for their wedding seventeen years ago. I'm not sure if she thinks it should go in a display case, or if she's under the impression that we should be serving spaghetti on it or what. Mostly it gets used when she borrows it for her book club meetings.

My mom just smiled. "No rush to bring it back."

"Bye, Mimi," I said, opening the door for her.

"Goodbye, sweetheart." I could smell her perfume as she gave me a peck on the cheek. My grandmother is classy, I'll give her that. I watched at the door as she placed the platter on the passenger seat of her silver Tesla, then went around to the driver's side, climbed in, and drove away.

With a sigh, I closed the door. "I'm heading upstairs to study," I said.

Mom was loading the dishwasher. "Okay, sweetie. I've got some emails, so I'll be down here at the table if you need me."

I went upstairs to my room and flopped onto my unmade bed. Yes, I'm organized. But I'm not very *tidy*. My social studies review sheets were scattered all over. I picked them up and placed them back in order so I could go through them again, then glanced out the window. Harry's bedroom is directly across from mine. I could see the back of his head shadowed against the bright lights from his monitor, where he was busily shooting some kind of military zombie things.

I pulled out my phone and typed, **start studying**.

A moment later, I saw him pause his game and reach for his phone. Then he was shooting again as the text came through: **stop stalking me**.

Grr.

Ten percent of our grade!

Through the window I saw Harry pick up his phone with one hand and then toss it across the room, onto his bed. Exasperated, I stood up and closed my blinds so that I wouldn't have to watch him play his ridiculous game instead of study.

I tried to look over my social studies notes, but I couldn't focus. Nothing is more annoying than someone leaving you on read. So I decided to text my sister:

Hey.

Hey!

Test tomorrow and I'm avoiding work

Oh ha ha I hear you.

Mimi was over

Getting the platter?

You're psychic

How can dad just ignore her?

Life experience.

Hows Greenwood?

Still good. Actually on an excursion at the mall—we're about to head into a movie. Dream Social?

Dream Society? I hear it's good

I'll let you know.

I sent a heart and that was it. Linden was out with her friends.

She's at a boarding school this year. Linden has problems with planning and following instructions, and middle school was kind of a disaster for her, grades-wise. So Mom decided that she should try a private school for high school, which meant that last year was crazy for both of them with applications and interviews and essays.

Anyway, the great news is that Linden got into Greenwood Academy, where she can get lots of support. And the campus looks like something out of a movie about a fancy college: sailboats, crew, golf(?!), excursions, amazing classes. All the teachers have PhDs and stuff.

There's a stable so kids can do dressage, which is where you sit on a horse and make it dance around and hop over fences. Apparently, it's an Olympic event, which is funny because the gold medal doesn't even go to the horse. I'm off topic, but the thing is, they always seem to have activities and stuff, which has been great for Linden because she's made a bunch of friends, but it's a bummer for me because I don't get to talk to her that much. It's been almost a full school year and I'm still not used to the fact that I can't just knock on the door across from mine and bother her whenever I feel like it.

I held up a page about the Mesopotamians. I didn't really feel like studying, but I really didn't want to get a bad grade, either. Ms. Dobbler is kind of a notoriously tough grader and I actually got an A-minus last semester, which means I'm in danger of sliding into B territory.

Harry and Monique both think that worrying about a B is dumb. The thing about Linden is that she never thinks that the stuff I worry about is dumb.

But she doesn't act like it's very serious, either.

She just knows how to get me to stay calm and focus . . .
like I needed to do at that moment.

The familiar creeping dread blobbed onto my toes. You
know that expression, *Getting cold feet*? Well, that actually
happens to me sometimes, and it happened then. The cold
spread up my legs and pooled in my stomach. I started
to feel vomitous . . . is *vomitous* a word? Well, that was how
I felt. I swallowed hard, forcing the nerves in my throat
back down into my stomach, then reached for my computer and opened it. *Focus*, I told myself. *Focus!* I could
study for three hours, then wake up early and reread the
worksheets. *I'll be okay*, I told myself. *I'll be okay*.

I'll just study, and I'll be okay.

CHAPTER TWO

Didaskaleinophobia—fear of school

Is it still a phobia if it's justified? Last year, Linden and I were both at the middle school, and Mom was *stressed*. She didn't think the school was helping Linden enough, and every time Linden brought home a report card, Mom would get mad and march down to the school to meet with Linden's teachers and Dr. Funk.

When Mom saw my first report card, with its string of As (and one A-), her eyes welled up with tears. I think she was relieved. Dad said, "Keep it up!" and that's what I'm trying to do.

Keep it up!

My eyes snapped open the next morning and I looked at the clock: 8:00 a.m.

How? Wait—I dimly remembered my phone going off at 6:30 a.m., as usual. I remember thinking, *One more minute*, and hitting the snooze button . . .

8:01!

I sat up in bed and immediately felt dizzy. I'd had a lot of trouble falling asleep because I was picturing my very bleak future. It had been a long, terrible night in my Barbie-pink room (I chose the color when I was five) as I imagined a very convincing worst-case scenario: flunking out of school, living with my parents, then having my parents get sick, die, then having the house get taken away by the government (is that a thing that can happen?), then living alone in a box with only a bedbug as a pet, then getting arrested, then going to prison and not even being allowed to bring along my pet bedbug. By three in the morning, I was practically crying just imagining saying goodbye to my beloved bug while a cruel guard made me shave off my hair (is that a thing that happens in prison?) while she laughed.

Now that I'd had two hours of sleep and the sun was up, I realized that this whole scenario was pretty unlikely, partly because I don't think I'd ever really have a pet bedbug. Like, they aren't even furry, and I've always said that if I ever had a pet, I'd want a fuzzy one. I wonder if I could take a plant to prison?

There was a knock at my door and a split-second later, my mom popped her head into my room. She looked confused. "You're just getting up?"

"I know, I know!" I said. "I had a rough night."

"Are you sick?" Pushing the door wide, she came in and placed her hand on my forehead. She was already dressed for work, in her "good pants" and a blue sweater that made the gray in her short dark hair shine like silver.

"I just . . . couldn't sleep," I admitted. "I was basically wide-awake from three to six. And now I feel a little nauseated."

"Hm." Mom frowned. "What's going on? Is this like Acapulco?"

"No," I said.

"What's going on?" Dad padded into the room, also dressed for work in a polo shirt, pajama bottoms, and slippers. He mostly works from home, so he only has to look presentable from the waist up. "Lizzie's sick?"

"It's like Acapulco," Mom said.

"Oh no!" Dad put on his sympathetic pout. "Your tummy hurts?"

Two weeks ago, we were on a family vacation in Mexico for spring break, and I'd bailed on a couple of our planned activities. Zip-lining and parasailing . . . I don't know— just the thought of them had made my stomach hurt. So Linden and Dad went parasailing and I stayed at the hotel with Mom, then Linden and Mom went zip-lining, and I stayed at the hotel with Dad, and both times it was fine.

I hung out at the pool and didn't need to throw up or anything. But ever since, Mom's been worried about my nervous stomach.

"Why don't you just stay home and rest today?" Dad suggested.

"I can't. I've got the test." This is a thing that both of my parents do—they act like school is optional, as if my grade doesn't depend on being in class and actually learning things and being tested on them. How am I supposed to "keep it up" if I stay home every time my stomach hurts? "I just didn't sleep well. I'll be fine."

"Why don't you try some deep breaths?" Mom suggested.

"They have meditation classes at Greenwood," Dad put in helpfully.

"Dad, I don't go to Greenwood," I snapped. "I go to Fuller Middle School—and I need to get there ASAP."

"Why don't you rest?" Dad suggested. "You can make up the test later."

I shook my head. "I'll fall behind."

"Linden always—"

"Mom, I'm not Linden, okay? I'd rather just get it over with!" Flinging back my covers, I stood up and went to my bureau to pull out clothes. Honestly, it was tempting to skip the test and make it up later. But I knew that would just mean an extra day of worrying and an extra sleepless night. Just the thought of it stressed me out even more!

"All right, all right..." Checking his phone, Dad retreated into the hallway, already absorbed in an email.

"I can drop you off on my way to work," Mom said. "And I'll make you a smoothie—you can drink it in the car."

"You're the best," I told her as I grabbed a pair of socks. I threw the clothes on my bed and had just started to take off my nightshirt when my mom paused at the door. I shrugged my arms back into my sleeves.

"Sweetie, I think maybe we should do something about how anxious you're feeling."

"I'm fine."

"It just seems like you've been worried a lot lately.

Maybe we can find some ways for you to relax and—"

"Mom, seriously. I don't have time for this right—"

"Okay, okay—I'll go make the smoothie," she said, shutting the door.

I stood there a moment, still in my nightshirt. *Does Mom think I worry more than most people? Don't lots of people get stressed when they have tests and stuff?*

Ugh, I didn't have time to think about it.

I'd think about it later, after the test.

And that was when I suddenly remembered the election.

Focus! I told myself. *You're only allowed to worry about one thing at a time!*

But it turns out that my brain is capable of lots of amazing things when it comes to being freaked out.

"Listen, I have an important question for you," Ant said as I scuttled into social studies with a pile of worksheets clutched to my chest.

"Do you want to look at my notes?" Sliding into my seat, I unzipped my backpack and reached for my notebook. I was still hoping to cram a few more facts into my brain before the test. "Here."

"What? No—I want to know who you would be if you could be anyone in the *Star Wars* universe." Ant held up his notebook, as if he were about to record my answer.

I blinked at him. "*That's* your important question?"

"Kylo Ren," Jacob Underhill put in.

"Man, you want to be the whiniest villain ever?" His best friend, Daneyal Khan, shook his head. "At least be Anakin."

"Or some kind of Sith Lord," Harry suggested from the seat in front of me.

"Okay, I'm trying to study for a test here." I waved a worksheet in their faces. "Please don't confuse me when I'm trying to remember Mesopotamian names like Gilgamesh and Enkidu."

"I'd be Rey," April McDonough said, and I rolled my eyes because she was probably right. April is good-looking and athletic, and has serious main-character energy. "Who would you be, Ant?" she asked.

"Jar Jar Binks," Ant announced, which made Jake laugh.

Dan rolled his eyes. "Man, you're twisted. Nobody wants to be Jar Jar."

"An Ewok, then. Hey, Ms. Dobbler!"

Our teacher, who was standing by the door to nod politely to students and check their names off the attendance list as they entered the classroom, turned her head to give Ant a cool look. "Yes?"

Ant cupped his hands around his mouth. "Who would you be if you could be anyone in the *Star Wars* universe?"

She blinked slowly in the way that lizards do. "Is your grade in my class really high enough for this?"

"It is *not*!" Ant said cheerfully. Then he turned to me, "Lizzie, pass me one of those worksheets."

"Where are yours?"

"Ewoks don't have time for worksheets," he said.

Shaking my head, I handed him one that I had already memorized. A moment later, Monique raced into class just as the bell rang and hurried over to me. "Lizzie! There you are!" she whispered as she ducked next to my desk. I reluctantly stopped silently reciting the hierarchy of Mesopotamian society.

"What's up?" I asked.

It had been pouring all morning. Even now, the classroom had that eerie lighting it has when the overhead fluorescents are on and the sky beyond the windows is dark with clouds. Monique's jacket and long braids were wet, and she looked like she was sweating, as if she had been racing around the school before the bell. Something had happened, I could tell. *Did she forget to study?*

"You weren't at your locker—"

"Something happening?" Harry asked, twisting around in his seat again.

"Excuse me, Monique, Harry, and Lizzie, but we have a test this morning," Ms. Dobbler said from the front of the classroom. "I'd like to see you all in your seats and facing forward."

I suddenly realized that Dobbler's *Star Wars* character

was obvious: She's basically the same age as Yoda and has the same legendary reputation. Oh yes, you will learn everything there is to know about ancient civilizations, because if you don't, she'll cut your arm off with a light-saber, metaphorically speaking. She's Yoda-sized, too: less than five feet tall, with short gray hair, pale skin, and black-framed glasses. In her tailored black pants and black sweater, she looks like she's ready to channel the dark side. Scary, she is.

Harry turned to face the front, while Monique hesitated, glancing from me to the teacher. Dobbler's huge black eyes slow-blinked behind her lenses.

"Now," she clarified in that tone that sounds like the exit door slamming.

Standing up, Monique turned and made her way to her seat. We have assigned seats in this class, which is super annoying. Ms. Dobbler mixes it up every two weeks. I guess she hopes we'll get to know new people and make friends and all of that stuff that teachers are always encour-aging us to do, but it really just means that we have to get out our phones if we want to tell our actual friends something.

Which is what Monique did. I felt my phone vibrate in my pocket. I made sure that Dobbler was busy at the other end of the room before I pulled it out.

It was a photo of April. Her golden curls were blowing in the breeze, and her teeth were even in a bright smile. White text over a red banner read: VOTE APRIL FOR 8TH-GRADE SECRETARY!

I know that it's normal to say something like "My blood ran cold" or "A tingle ran down my spine" when you feel freaked out. But when I get a bad surprise, I really do feel like I've swallowed an ice cube; like there's a hunk of snow right in the center of my chest that somehow radiates to my armpits and makes me start to sweat. I know that's gross and not poetic, but it's the truth. I'm a very moist worrier—it's always tears, perspiration, or waves of nausea with me.

If I had to come up with worst-case scenarios about who the absolute worst person to be running against for class secretary, April would probably be the whole list. She's pretty, she's got great hair, she's artsy, and people like her. She'd definitely be Rey, while I'd be one of those droids in the background.

I looked over at Monique, who was texting away.

The three little dots blinked on my screen and finally revealed the next text: **Don't worry we will crush her**

The chunk of ice in my chest shifted, like it was trying to grow and spread throughout my entire torso. Somehow, the idea of trying to "crush" anyone in the election was even more terrifying than just having competition. I'd just wanted to run unopposed! Now I was supposed to crush someone?

"Monique?" Dobbler had noticed she was texting. "All phones away; we're about to start."

Monique looked over at me, mashing her lips together and narrowing her eyes as she put away her phone. Then she nodded and made a fist.

Oh no. The thing about Monique is that she isn't afraid to get into it. She could easily turn this election for secretary into a brawl—and she already couldn't stand April.

Of course my brain wasted no time getting to work on this new situation. *Monique makes a campaign poster for me that insults April. April gets mad and they get into a shouting match. I step between them just as April takes out a lightsaber—*

"You may begin," Dobbler announced.

Shake it off, I told myself.

I turned over the paper and wrote my name at the top. Then I looked at the first question, but I could hardly concentrate. I had to force myself not to write down "April McDonough" as the answer to every question.

The ice in my chest started to melt, dripping into my stomach and pooling there. Glancing at Harry's back, I saw that he was bent over his paper, filling in answers.

I tried to focus on my test. Name the character who was Gilgamesh's best friend. *Ahsoka*, I thought. *No—not Ahsoka. Anakin. Obi-Wan Kenobi? No, wait . . .*

I could only think of *Star Wars* characters! My heart was throbbing.

Admiral Ackbar. Andor. Boba Fett.

Gah! The gears in my mind were jammed. April . . . and Ant . . . had jammed them.

$$\mathcal{C}\!\!\nearrow$$

"So, sweetie, I managed to talk to a few people and I read a few articles over lunch," Mom said as she peeled a carrot. She's so good at peeling carrots that the peels fly off and collect into a bowl as she does it. I hope I never get that good at peeling carrots because I'm willing to bet that the only way to get that good is to peel a horrifying number of carrots.

"What are you talking and reading about?" I asked. Our kitchen, dining area, and living room are one large L-shaped space, and I was setting the table as Mom got dinner ready. Dad was on the couch, as usual. He's a terrible cook, so he's in charge of dishwashing, which means that he's usually on the couch working right up until dinner.

"What we talked about this morning—adolescent anxiety," Mom replied.

"We talked about adolescent anxiety?"

"Ho-*ney,*" she said, putting extra emphasis on that second syllable, "of course! You were so anxious this morning that you almost missed school!" Shaking her head, she dumped the carrot peels into the compost bucket.

"Oh, that," I said. "I was just worried about my test."

"But that's unusual for you."

"It is?"

Mom turned to face me. "You don't usually worry about school," she said.

"That's not true," I told her. "Last year was really hard—all of the changing classes, and tons more homework than fifth grade! I was worried a lot in sixth grade, and last semester was even harder."

"Really?" Mom put down the peeler. "You never said." Her eyebrows drew together, and I wondered if she was feeling guilty that she hadn't realized how hard adjusting to middle school had been for me.

"I mean . . . I just dealt with it. Like I did this morning, with the test."

"How did it go?"

"Ugh, pretty badly . . ."

"Did you study?" This was from my dad. At some point, he had looked up from his computer screen and joined the conversation.

"Of *course* I studied," I snapped.

"Then the teaching wasn't good." Dad closed his laptop and set it aside. "Francine, I'm starting to have my doubts about that school."

"I don't think the school is the problem. The problem is Lizzie's anxiety."

"The school was *not* fine for Linden," Dad shot back.

"Fuller is fine—it's a good school," I said quickly.

"But are they really setting you up for success in high school?" Dad asked.

"Yes! And next year is going to be even better." Everyone knows that eighth grade is the best year at Fuller. There's the class trip, and Dobbler teaches a world mythology class that I'm dying to take. It's really hard to get into, which is part of the reason I want to do well in her class this year.

"Look, sweetie, you've been very anxious lately." Mom turned back to her carrots and started slicing. "You've always been my little worrywart, but I think maybe it's time to brainstorm ways we can help you relax. I'm going to try to find you a therapist, but everyone says that they're nearly impossible to get now, so in the meantime, we should think about the mind-body connection. I think we need to eat really healthily and maybe you should get more exercise, which will help your sleep—"

"I hate sportsy things," I said. Anything with a ball and/or running around is just . . . not for me. I'm slow, I'm uncoordinated—I'm not like Monique, who's great at all that stuff, or Harry, who could be but would rather shoot imaginary zombies.

"You need to do something besides academics," Dad added. "You need more activities—more new people. You can't just hang around with the same two friends you've had since kindergarten." He opened his laptop again.

I've heard this speech from him before. "I'm running for class secretary," I said.

But I'd already lost his attention. His eyes were back on his screen, his mind obviously back at work.

Mom heard me, though. "You are? That's wonderful!"

I knew she'd like that.

"But you also need exercise."

"Are there any exercises that are, like, not a sport?" I asked.

"You don't have to play a sport or join a team," Mom said. "You could just go for a walk."

"I do that," I replied. "Sometimes."

"Well, you should be doing it for half an hour a day," Mom said.

"Walking is good for you." Dad was suddenly part of the conversation again.

"And what about a dog?" Mom suggested.

"Now, that's a good idea," Dad agreed. "Dog walking!" The timer went off and Mom pulled a sheet pan of chicken and roasted potatoes from the oven as Dad added, "You could earn a little spending money."

Mom tossed the carrot bits onto the pan and put it back

in the oven. "You know, we've never really considered this whole dog idea," she said.

"Linden always wanted a dog," I said. "But you and Dad said no."

"You two were younger then. But pets are supposed to be excellent for relieving anxiety. People even have therapy dogs."

"There you go." Dad nodded at Mom. "Great point."

"I mean . . . I do like dogs," I admitted as I filled up the water pitcher. I wasn't so sure I loved the idea of starting a business, though. Would I put up flyers or something? With my name on them? So embarrassing. "But how do I do it? Could you ask around?"

"Oh, I think Maryellen knows someone close by who has a dog. She's actually looking for someone," Mom agreed. "I'll text her!"

"Go for it," Dad said.

With a sigh, I placed the yellow pitcher on the table. "How much time until dinner?" I asked.

Mom looked at her watch. "Eleven minutes."

"Cool; I'll be back," I said as I headed upstairs to my room, feeling a little overwhelmed. I wasn't really sure that I wanted to start dog walking at the exact same time that I was running for class secretary. *Then again, Mom might have a point*, I thought. The actual walking part would be kind of fun and relaxing . . . and I would earn some money. I had met Mom's friend Maryellen. She was kind of loony but very nice. So maybe she'd know of some low-stress after-school gig.

Then again, I might not be able to do it after school every day, I realized, *because I'll probably have meetings for class government. If I win. If I lose, I'll have plenty of time.*

My heart squeezed like a fist. *What if I lose? Then I'll really need something to do.*

I pulled my phone out of my back pocket. **Did Sascha ever walk dogs?** I typed.

Three dots . . . then Linden replied. **I think so.**

How did she get people?

I don't know.

I waited for Linden to say that she would text her best friend and ask, but she didn't. So I typed, **Would you ask her?**

Sure.

And then, like, nothing. No more dots. I mean, I guess she didn't need to ask anything, really, like *Oh, are you interested in walking dogs?* Because that was kind of obvious. But still. Didn't Linden want to talk to me?

I'm running for class secretary, I wrote.

You'll be good at that!

April's running, too, I'm worried I'll lose to her

Don't worry. You got this.

And . . . dotless. She was done.

She's probably at dinner, I realized. I knew the dining

hall was pretty hectic—we ate there once when we drove out to visit Linden for family day. This is probably a bad time.

I sighed. For some reason, nobody was really worried about me losing to April. Nobody but me.

CHAPTER THREE

A Partial List of Things That Freak Me Out:

Cottage cheese, snakes, dentists, dental instruments, other people's bathrooms, random hairs on things, feet, clowns that are interacting with the audience (clowns engaged in juggling and/or exiting a tiny car are okay), loud noises, rearview mirrors that stick way out on the side of buses and might hit the back of my head as I walk down the sidewalk, pigeons, wasps, any ant larger than a sesame seed, ticks, creepy demon children in movies

(I can't even watch trailers for that stuff), puppets that are not on television, historical reenactors, blobby fat on a piece of chicken, failing out of school, spiders, lobsters that are still alive and in a tank desperate to be free, karaoke, crowds, guns, being forced to make a speech in front of the class, tsunamis, tornadoes, and April McDonough.

Of course.

April stabbed Monique the minute I opened the door to the gym. The buzzer went off and Monique groaned in frustration.

"Keep focus," Coach Yao called. The rest of the fencing team was seated. There were a few other kids from school—Noah Adams, Amaya Pranang, and Andy Yun—sitting on the bench, watching April and Monique with their foils. The thing about fencing is that you have to wear a full suit of protective gear and a mesh face mask, but even with all of that I could tell which one is Monique because of how she moves. Also because she gets furious when anyone gets a point on her.

Monique ripped off her mask and glared at the scoreboard. She glanced at me as I took a seat on the far end of the bench, then shoved her mask back onto her head and stood in the ready position, shifting her weight between her front and back foot, prepared to pounce.

Across from her, April stood perfectly still, like a bird about to take flight.

At the signal, they faced off. Monique danced forward and they crossed foils. Then dance, dance, and Monique lunged, stabbing April in the chest. And that was it. Monique pulled off her mask again, and I could tell by the look on her face that she had won.

She and April shook hands as Coach Yao turned to everyone on the bench. "Great practice, everybody," she said. "I'll see you next Wednesday."

"Great . . . slicing!" I told Monique as she walked up to me.

"Thanks," she said. "We can head out in two minutes. Let me just put away my gear. Oh, crap . . ."

April was walking over to us, smiling. She had taken off her mask to reveal a sweaty face and lopsided ponytail. Out of the corner of my eye, I could see that Noah was watching her. *Still got that crush*, I thought. *Poor Noah.*

"Great job, Monique," April said brightly.

"Thanks." Monique glanced over at Coach Yao, who was watching. "You did well, too," she added in a grudging voice.

"Hi, Lizzie." April turned to me and cocked her head. "Is it true that you're running for class secretary, too?"

"Yep."

"Wow! Really?" April was holding a long navy-blue bag, and she shoved her foil inside as she talked, smiling the whole time. "When Ant told me, I didn't even believe him. I know you hate putting yourself out there."

Before I could say anything (not that I would have; I seriously had no idea how to reply to that), Monique said, "Oh, she'll be out there. I'm her campaign manager."

April lifted an eyebrow, as if she doubted it. "Cool." Then there was a moment of awkward standing around before April added, "Well, my mom is here, so . . ." She tossed her ponytail and strode off.

"Come back," Monique muttered as April disappeared. "I want to stab you some more."

"Monique, come on—let's go."

She finished taking off her gear, said goodbye to the coach and waved to Noah and Amaya and we headed to the bagel and smoothie place that we really like—Bagel Town—which is close to school.

"Okay," Monique said once we were on the sidewalk. "How about this as a campaign slogan: Vote Lizzie! She's Not Phony and Passive-Aggressive, Unlike April."

"Seems long," I replied.

"Okay, how about, April Will Stab You in the Front *and* the Back. Do You Really Want That? Vote Lizzie!"

"These . . . need work."

"April Bad, Lizzie Good!"

That actually made me laugh. "I think maybe we shouldn't go negative."

"Oh, ugh!" Monique rolled her eyes, but she was smiling. "I want to get to the *crushing*."

"Let's not talk about her at all," I suggested, mostly because even the sound of April's name makes me feel squirmy. "I don't even want to think about her."

Monique came to a dead stop in front of Bagel Town. "You're right," she agreed. "April is a nonfactor. We're focused on the Lizzie campaign. Whatever *she* does doesn't affect us at all."

I took a deep breath. "I think that's the best way."

With a nod, Monique yanked open the glass door, releasing a blast of air-conditioning that hit me like the wave of relief I was feeling.

The café was bustling. I ordered a berry blast smoothie, and Monique got her usual—a cinnamon raisin bagel with peanut butter, which sounded kind of gross to me the first time I heard it but is actually good.

"I'm getting water. Want some?" I asked.

"Definitely," Monique said. "I'll grab us a table."

The minute I saw the line at the self-serve watercooler, though, I turned and joined Monique at the table, which she was wiping down with napkins. (She hates crumbs.)

"No water?" she asked.

"Rex Heartson," I hissed, slipping into my chair.

We both swiveled our heads to look. Rex was standing at the end of the watercooler line, looking down so his black bangs dipped over one eye, scrolling on his phone. Absently, he raked his hand through his hair, smoothing it for a moment before it dropped back into place.

Monique poked me in the shoulder. "This is your chance."

She knows I've had a crush on him since last year, when I stayed after English class to talk to Ms. Haye and he thought that I had come early for some mountain bike club meeting that was happening in the same room. He was really nice and friendly and acted like I'd be a huge asset to the mountain bike club (he clearly had no clue that I'm the least athletic person ever) and I felt so embarrassed having to tell him that I was just there to meet a teacher. But he just said, "Too bad!" and looked disappointed and smiled a dreamy smile and ever since then I have avoided talking to him again because he makes me feel like I'm about to have a heart attack.

"I can't do it," I insisted.

"You're impossible." Monique shook her head.

"I can't!"

"I should haul you over there, but I'm too thirsty after that practice. *I'll* get the water."

I watched as Rex slipped his phone into his back pocket, filled one glass, then another. As he turned away from the dispenser, he nearly ran into Monique. He smiled and said something. She said something back and he laughed, and I nearly ripped the edge of the table off, I was squeezing it so hard.

Someone in a black apron blocked my view. "Berry smoothie and cinnamon raisin?"

"Uh, yeah." The server placed the plate and drink in front of me, and Monique was already back with our waters.

"What was that? What happened?" I demanded as she put down the glasses and plopped into her seat.

Monique gave me a smug little smile and then took a bite of her peanut butter–topped bagel and chewed. And chewed. And chewed—all while I was about to pass out and curse the invention of peanut butter.

"What did he say? Tell me!"

She swiped daintily at the corners of her mouth and blinked innocently. "Who?"

"I will stab you with this straw," I threatened.

She laughed. "Nothing! He said, 'Oops,' because he almost tripped over my foot. And I said, 'Don't spill that water.' And then he said, 'Yeah, I'm really thirsty.'" Monique tilted her head, imitating Rex, and mimed holding up two glasses. "And then I got out two glasses and said, 'Me too.' And then we both smiled and he went and sat with Jeremy Jakes at that little table in the back corner."

I sat back in my chair. "Oh, wow."

She shrugged. "It could have been you."

"Do you think he knows who you are?" I asked, trying

to sneak a peek at the table in the back. Unfortunately, it's almost completely hidden by the counter. I could only see the back of Rex's hair and the edge of his backpack.

"No, but I think he realized we're at the same school."

"Is that seriously all you said to each other? He was laughing!"

"He's just really nice, Lizzie," Monique said. "Neither one of us said anything remotely cool or interesting."

I took a sip of my smoothie, barely tasting it.

"It *should* have been you," Monique went on. "Next time, it will be."

I sighed. "I don't know."

"You can definitely make stupid jokes about water as well as I can."

"Really?"

"Please don't act like this is some kind of compliment. All you have to do is stand there and be nice so that Rex knows who you are! It's not rocket science. It isn't even pushing the button to make the rocket go up in the air. It's just, like, standing there and smiling at a rocket so that the rocket knows you exist." She took a ferocious bite of her bagel.

"I think that metaphor kind of went off the rails at the end."

Monique's mouth was stuffed, so she just pointed at me and narrowed her eyes. I got the message: *Woman up and be a little brave.*

Monique doesn't get that it's a lot easier for her—she isn't afraid of anything, while I'm afraid of many, many things. Bravery isn't so easy for someone like me.

I walked home thinking about that interaction the whole way. My brain supplied a series of images: Monique and Rex chatting at Bagel Town, then bumping into each other at school and laughing, then Monique walking to school in the rain and Rex running to catch up with her and offering her an umbrella (I saw this in a movie once), then Rex asking her out and then, finally, an image of myself many years in the future, dressed in an ugly bridesmaid dress at their wedding.

I can't draw, dance, or sing, but I'm very creative when it comes to imagining far-fetched nightmare scenarios.

I wish there was a way to make money at it, instead of just giving myself a stomachache.

I noticed that both of our cars were in the driveway, which was weird because Mom almost never gets home before five thirty on a Wednesday. Naturally, my first thought was that she got fired (thanks, creative brain!) so I hurried to the side door and pushed it open, calling, "I'm home!"

"Sweetie!" Mom shouted, but I didn't even see her because a black-and-white dog was bounding over to me and jumping up, leaning on my hips with her paws. "Meet Bella!"

"Hi, Bella!" I squatted to give the dog a pet as Mom hurried over and grabbed her by the collar. "Is this . . ." I noticed that Dad was standing in the middle of the living room, wearing a face-sized frown. "Is this for my dog-walking job?"

"No," Mom said with a grin. "She's our dog!"

"What?" I stared at Bella, who was gazing at me with huge hazel eyes and panting happily. The sides of her head were black and her ears pointed straight up, like she was wearing a Batman mask. But there was a blaze of white that ran down the front of her face and around her muzzle, interrupted only by her black nose. "Oh my gosh!" I leaned in to hug her, and she gave me a lick on the cheek.

"I don't know about this," Dad grumbled.

"This was your idea, Gerald!" Mom planted her hands on her hips.

"*My* idea?"

"How did this even happen?" I asked.

"What do you mean?" Mom demanded, pulling off her red blazer and slinging it across the back of one of our dining chairs. "I told you that Maryellen had a friend with a dog who needed a home, and Daddy said to go for it . . ."

"I said that Lizzie should walk dogs," Dad insisted. "Not own one."

"Gerald! You can't be serious—I said that we could get

a therapy dog and you said, 'Go for it,' and I said, 'Great, I'll text Maryellen!'"

"I never said that!"

"That is a *direct quote*!"

"I was saying that Lizzie should walk dogs because she could earn a little money." He turned to me. "Lizzie, back me up here."

I was busy scratching Bella behind the ears. She jutted her chin forward and her eyes slowly closed. "I mean . . . I agree that I thought we were talking about me walking other people's dogs," I admitted. "But look at this face!" I held Bella's face in my hands.

"See?" Mom said. "Dogs are relaxing! Look at them together. Aww."

Dad huffed out a frustrated sigh. "I never said we should get a dog. They're so much work!"

"But I'll be forced to get exercise," I pointed out. "Which Mom says will be good for my sleep and brain and whatever." I put my face beside Bella's. "Aren't we cute?"

"Oh, Gerald, I really thought you said we should get a

dog!" I could hear the worry creeping into Mom's voice. "And Bella needs a home . . ."

Dad looked suspicious. "Why? What's wrong with her?"

"Nothing—her owner passed away, so she's been in foster care with Maryellen's friend for a few weeks."

"Oh, that's so sad," I said, giving Bella another hug.

Dad walked over to the couch and plopped down. "Well . . ." I could feel him watching me and Bella, but I was busy giving her more scratches at the base of her tail, which she really seemed to like. Dropping to the floor, she rolled around on her back, wiggling wildly. "What, exactly, are we going to do if this dog is not relaxing?"

"Dogs are relaxing." Mom sounded certain.

"That's ridiculous; not all dogs are relaxing!" Dad insisted. "Some dogs are stressful! And if this dog isn't relaxing, then she'll have to go back to where she came from." I guess my face must have showed how horrified I was at this, because Dad's voice softened when he added, "I guess we can see how it goes. Is she house-trained?"

"Of course! And she sleeps in her own bed and

everything." Mom gestured to the dining table, which was covered in dog stuff—a bed, a stuffed frog, a tennis ball, two metal bowls, and a blue leash.

"Can I take her for a walk?" I asked. I wanted to get out of the house. I didn't want to hear any more of Dad's rant about the dog—it was starting to freak me out. There were too many worst-case scenarios, and I didn't want to start imagining them. "I want to show Harry."

"I'll come with you," Mom said.

"Oh, for heaven's sake, Francie, let her take the dog out herself. It's going to be her responsibility."

Mom showed me that the poop bags were attached to the leash in a bone-shaped container. Then I clipped the leash to Bella's collar, making a mental note that we should get a harness.

"Dinner at six thirty," Mom called as Bella and I headed out the side door.

Bella was good on a leash. She didn't try to pull me around or anything, just trotted right by my side as we walked down the driveway. She did stop to sniff a clump of purple crocus flowers, but when I said, "Come on, Bella," she followed me.

At Harry's house, she bounded up the three steps at the end of his concrete walkway. Harry's mom keeps their yard looking great. She had planted a bunch of daffodils on either side of the path, and she had put a whole spring display on the porch: a bunch of tin buckets filled with pansies, three stone rabbits, and a cheerful sign that read BLOOM WHERE YOU ARE PLANTED in curly script. I guess she's one of those people who spends a lot of time at Michael's. My mom doesn't care about that stuff—we're lucky if she remembers to take the Christmas wreath down by June—and my dad doesn't really get holidays. I was happy to see that Bella trotted past all of it without trampling the flowers or digging into the buckets.

I texted Harry that I was outside with a surprise, and a minute later, I heard footsteps on the stairs and then the door swung open. "What's the—oh, wow, who's this?" Harry bent over to pet Bella, who wagged.

"We have a dog now!"

"Wait, what?" Harry looked up at me.

"This is Bella." We sat on the porch steps and I told him all about what happened, imitating my mom's excitement, my dad's disapproval, and then my mom's worry. Harry found the whole misunderstanding hilarious.

He grabbed a jacket and we started down the street, on our usual route.

"So is this dog making you more relaxed?" Harry asked.

"Well, she seems like a good dog," I said.

"I haven't heard you mention the social studies test."

"Why did you have to bring up the social studies test?"

"Oh my gosh." Harry covered his face with his hands. "Why did I say that?"

I shook my head. "I have no idea how I did."

"You did fine. You always do fine. You always freak out and then do fine. It's kind of annoying."

"It's annoying?" We stopped for a moment as Bella carefully sniffed a blade of grass.

Harry's eyes went wide. "I mean, not to *me*. But it might be annoying to people who don't do well on the test."

"Oh no, do you think they're not going to vote for me for class secretary?"

"What? Is that what—oh my gosh, how does your brain work? Lizzie, get a grip." Harry laughed and pulled a bright green leaf from a low branch and twirled it between his fingers.

"You just said I was annoying!"

"Bella, make her relax, would you?" Bella cocked her head in an effort to understand what Harry was saying. "Oh, you're cute." He gave her a pat. "Don't you find *this* relaxing?"

"It *is* cute," I admitted. "You're so cute, Bella!"

We pet the dog some more and told her how adorable she is. Then we walked through the black iron gates that led to the cemetery. "How do you think you did on the test?" I asked Harry.

"It's anyone's guess." Harry's a bit of a wild card when it comes to school. He's smart, but—as you know—he doesn't love to study.

We walked in silence for a while, the only sound the

crunch of gravel beneath our feet and Bella sniffing at things.

I looked at my watch. "I have to be home by six thirty."

"Okay. We'll turn around in a minute. But listen, I have news."

I looked at him dubiously. "Is it about gaming?"

"How did you know?" Harry looked shocked.

"You only have one hobby."

"Okay, yes. It's about gaming, but even you might find it interesting. I've scored high enough to play in a first-round elimination match of *Zombiesquad*!"

He was clearly so excited that my heart actually started to beat faster and I said, "Cool!" before I realized that I didn't have a clue what he was talking about. "Wait, what does that mean?"

"It means that I'm going to play against twenty other people who scored really high on *Zombiesquad*, and if I win, I get to actually enter the tournament. It's usually just for professionals."

I hadn't even realized that there were professional

gamers until about eight months ago, when Harry showed me a live tournament with actual crowds of people watching, like with other sportsy stuff. "Are you going to be live—in person somewhere?"

"No, no, that's only for the final rounds. I'll probably get eliminated way before that. But I'll get to play with those guys, real pros who're the best—"

And then we heard a sneeze.

"It's me!" Ant called. He was walking toward us and waving. "Don't be scared! Oh my gosh, who is this?" And he immediately forgot about us and started petting Bella. "Who is this? Is this a good dog? Is this the bestest dog?"

"This is Bella," I said.

"Bella! The *bella* Bella! *Bella* means beautiful in Spanish. Perfect name for a perfect dog!" As he straightened up, we could see Ant's enormous grin. "Is she yours?" he asked Harry.

"Mine," I said.

"You're so lucky! My parents won't let me get a dog. So what's up? How did the test go?"

I groaned as Harry said, "We're trying not to mention it around here." He made a cutting motion across his throat with his hand, then jerked his head in my direction.

Ant nodded knowingly. "Don't worry, I'm sure you did great. You always do."

That made me wonder if Ant was one of the people who thought it was annoying when I worried about my grades. But I didn't ask. Instead, we just compared answers on questions number nine and seventeen, and then Ant said he had to get going.

"Should we head home, too?" Harry asked.

"I just want to go a tiny bit farther," I said, and pivoted to the right, in the direction Ant came from.

We passed the crypt he had been lying on the first night we ran into him. It belonged to the Polycyzek family and looked ancient, so I scanned the other tombstones nearby. "Why do you think we keep running into Ant?"

Harry pursed his lips. "I don't know. Maybe he's wondering why he keeps running into us." But Harry stopped in his tracks and seemed to consider for a moment. Then he strode over to the crypt, which was built into the side of a small hill. He hauled himself up the green and stood on top, looking out. "You can see Miller Field from here," he said.

That's the big, empty space that's usually filled with soccer players on weekends. "Isn't that where—"

"Ant and Nico lit those firecrackers," Harry finished. Ant and Nico used to be best friends. But after that day in fifth grade when they'd been fooling around with fireworks and Ant had almost ended up blind in one eye, Nico's parents sent him to private school. I saw him around sometimes, but not very often.

"Do you think that's it?"

"What, that he's looking out over the field and contemplating where his life took a semi-dramatic turn?" Frowning, Harry shook his head. "I have no idea. Maybe he just likes crypts. Maybe he's a crypt keeper. Oh! Maybe his family changed their name from Polycyzek to Gutierrez, and this is his family crypt! All I know is that you said you had to get home by six thirty and we've got about seven minutes left."

"Yeah," I said. "We'd better go. Come on, Bella."

She was sniffing at a headstone—small, about the size of a brick—that was nearly hidden by a fading marigold plant. I leaned closer and read the name: ANTONIO TORRES.

Different last names. But Ant . . . and Antonio? It could be a coincidence.

But I wondered if *this* was why we kept running into Ant in the graveyard.

CHAPTER FOUR

A Totally Normal Conversation with My Dog

Bella: [looks up at me]

Me: Are you okay down there? Is that bed comfortable? You don't look comfortable. What if I move your bed on top of my bed? Is that good? Would you like that? [brief struggle as I get Bella to step off her bed, move her bed to the foot of my bed, then pat my bed for her to come up] Come on up here! Come on! Oh. No, wait, you're supposed to go lay down in your bed. *Your* bed. Your bed is here. You—oh, okay, you want to make a little nest? You want to dig under the covers? Okay, well—uh—is there room for me? Can I scooch in here? It's just...[struggles to push dog over] Are you actually making yourself heavier right now? Are you an X-Man with, like, special extra-weight powers? [struggles more] Okay. I know Dad said no dogs on the bed, but you're not on *his* bed so it's fine. You comfy? Oh, you—thank you for that kiss. Don't worry about Dad. He always says no to things and complains about them, and then if you just do them anyway, he ends up liking them. That's just kind of his thing. It stresses Mom out because she always wants everyone to be happy all the time. Which is kind of its own problem, you know?

Bella: [slowly closes eyes]

Me: I hope you like living with us. It used to be more fun when my sister, Linden, was here. Everyone likes Linden; she's everyone's favorite. And you're everyone's favorite, too! Harry thought you were great. And Ant seemed to like you.

Bella: [snores]

Me: Oh, yeah, sure. It's time to sleep now. I'm tired, too. Well, good night, Bella.

❧

"Did you take more pictures for me?" Monique calls from across the busy hallway. It's the usual one-minute-before-first-bell mayhem—a couple of seventh graders sitting on the floor in front of their lockers, copying each other's homework; Lila Montgomery and her eighth-grade group of dramaramas singing a Disney song; a clump of sixth-grade boys comparing drawings of dragons; and everyone else busily pulling things out of lockers, shoving things into lockers, slamming lockers, or shuffling slowly in groups of twos or threes in the vague direction of their first-period classes. And over all that, Monique was still yelling, "I need more dog content!"

She came bounding over and I got a better look at her vintage Hulk graphic tee, stylishly ripped jeans, and green converse sneakers. Her braids were piled into a bun on top of her head in a green scrunchie, and she had made dangly earrings out of two green army men. If I had tried to pull off that outfit, people would have been giving me weird looks. But Monique always manages to look amazing, and there's a whole group of sixth-grade girls who seem to worship her style. They'll probably all be wearing earrings made out of plastic toys by the end of the week.

I pulled out my phone and searched through my photos.

"Oh, that is so cute!" Monique said, leaning over my screen. "You let her sleep on your pillow?"

"I *tried* to get her to sleep on her own bed," I said, which was technically true.

"She's snuggled right up to you!"

"She's really sweet."

"I can't wait to meet her! Aww, look at this derp face!" In the picture, Bella was up on two legs with her eyes wide and her tongue hanging out.

"Yeah, I'd just given her a treat," I said.

"Who's a derp?" someone asked from behind us, and when I turned to see who it was, I nearly passed out. April McDonough was standing there. "Did you get a dog?" she asked Monique.

"It's Lizzie's dog."

"I didn't know you liked dogs."

"Everyone likes dogs, April." Monique folded her arms across her chest.

"Sure, but I know Lizzie's afraid of a lot of—" April stopped and shrugged.

Monique sighed dramatically and rolled her eyes.

"I'm not scared of dogs," I said.

"That's surprising," April said.

"April, why don't you just keep walking?" Monique suggested. "Go find your little clique and talk about whatever it is that you talk about."

They looked at each other for what felt like a length of time roughly equivalent to the Mesozoic Era (186 million years, according to earth science class). Then the bell rang, and April hitched her bag higher onto her shoulder and took off down the hall.

"That was horrifying," I said.

"Really?" Monique cocked her head and smiled, batting her eyelashes. "I enjoyed it."

"You don't think you were a little mean?" I asked.

"Of course not!" Monique hitched her backpack higher on her shoulder. "I was *very* mean."

I laughed as we started walking toward social studies. Sometimes, I really wish I could say whatever is on my mind, the way Monique does. I'm seriously in awe of her. But I also can't stand to see people's feelings hurt.

"Maybe April isn't as bad as we think," I said. "Everyone else seems to like her."

"That's because she's only rude to certain people. 'When someone shows you who they are, believe them.' Maya Angelou said that. The writer."

"The one your mom loves?"

"Exactly. That's my mom's favorite quote. She says it all the time, and it's true."

"You don't think people can change?"

"I think they *can* change," Monique said. "But they usually don't."

As we slipped into our seats in social studies, I noticed a stack of papers on Dobbler's desk. She graded our tests already? My heart started to pound.

"Hey, guess what," Harry said, turning around in his chair. He pulled back his sleeve.

"What happened to your arm?" I asked. It was covered in red welts.

"I think I'm allergic to your dog," he said.

"What? That's horrible," I said, but I couldn't stop

staring at the tests. A moment later, the second bell rang, and everyone settled into place. Finally, Ms. Dobbler stepped to the front of the room. She looked out over the class and did not smile.

"Did it just get cold in here?" Ant asked.

Picking up the stack of tests, she read out a name. "Jacob Underhill," she read, and Jake scurried up. He looked at his test, and I could tell from his expression that it hadn't gone well for him.

I tried to will my heart into beating normally as, one by one, everyone got their results. Nobody looked happy.

"Elizabeth Morris-Artino?" Ms. Dobbler always uses our full names, and sometimes it takes me a while to remember that Elizabeth is me.

I tried—and failed—to read her expression as I plucked the test from her hand.

Scrawled at the top and circled in red ink was a C+.

A C? I blinked at it. My heart felt like a balloon that had been filled too full—stretched and stretched and then—pop! Limp. I know that, for some people, a C is fine. It's normal. It's average. But I had never gotten below an A—in my life—and I had studied!

Once all the tests had been handed out, Dobbler crossed her arms. "I'm very disappointed," she said quietly.

Jake let out half a laugh before our teacher's stare stole the sound from his throat. The room was dead silent. I felt like I'd just fallen into a hole.

"I haven't entered the scores into GradeHub yet, because I'd like to give you all a chance to earn some extra credit," she went on. "I'm assigning a group project to be finished by next Wednesday."

Relief washed over me. *Extra credit! I could at least work my way up to a B . . . probably.* Monique and I made eye contact. *I'll work with Monique and maybe Ravi Singh or Estella Lopez. Ravi is supersmart, but his usual crowd of friends is in the other social studies section. And Estella is a hard worker, but very shy. Harry could maybe join us, too, although he's often not great on group projects . . .*

"Please listen carefully while I announce the groups," Dobbler said, and I felt like the hole I'd fallen into had just dropped into yet another hole. She was *assigning* the groups?

Jake and Dan were the first two called. They high-fived, and a moment later, Dobbler called Cecily VonAdams's name.

I felt sorry for her. I'd hate to have to work with those guys.

Monique's group was Mandy Wilson and Estella.

There goes that dream, I thought as Monique flashed me a disappointed look. A moment later, Dobbler called, "Hariko Sugihara? You're working with Elizabeth Morris-Artino . . ."

Okay, I'm with Harry, I thought. *That's okay. Come on, Ravi. Ravi, Ravi, Ravi—*

". . . and Antonio Gutierrez."

"All right!" Ant said. "I'm with Lizzie? I'm getting an A!"

The look Dobbler hurled at him was like a snowball—but not like a fun snowball, more like the kind that's hard as a rock and explodes in your face. "Everyone has to contribute to the group," she said. "If I suspect that one person is doing more work than the other group members, I'll simply divide that one person's grade into three parts."

"So . . . wait . . . what does that mean?" Ant asked.

"I'm going to average your grade for this project with your grade on the test. That means that you'll have earned a thirty-three percent, and your overall grade on the test will go down instead of up."

Ant frowned. "That doesn't sound like extra credit."

"Think of it as a second chance, then. A bonus assignment. And don't blow it."

In the seat in front of me, Harry ran his hands through his hair. I took a deep breath.

For once, I felt like the stress I was feeling wasn't just mine. The whole class felt nauseated.

"I'm home!" I called as I set down my bag by the side door and kicked off my shoes. What sounded like a herd of fifty dogs came bounding down the stairs, and a moment later, I was being greeted by a black-and-white wagging tornado.

"Hi, Bella! Hi! Hi! Did you have a good day?"

Dad appeared on the stairs.

"How'd it go with Bella?"

"She was fine," he said, sounding somewhat surprised as he stepped into the living room. "I put the dog bed under my desk and she just slept at my feet for most of the day." Bella walked over to him and wagged. "This is a good dog." He gave her a halting little pat on the head and she sat up on her hind legs. "What's this?"

"Oh, that's so cute! She looks like a meerkat!"

"Why is she doing this?" Dad asked. Have I mentioned that he's not really a pet guy?

"Give her a treat," I said.

"No, I'm not giving her a treat. If I give her a treat, then she'll expect me to give her treats."

"She already seems to expect you to give her treats, Dad," I said, heading for the counter. We'd had the dog less than twenty-four hours, but somehow, my mother had already put out a cookie jar that read DOG BISCUITS on the side and had a handle in the shape of a bone, so I took one out. The minute Bella saw me head for the jar, she came and did the little meerkat trick for me. I held the treat out gently, and she took it delicately from my palm.

"Let's go for a walk," I said, and Bella trotted over to the coat rack, where I'd hung up her leash the night before.

Dad shook his head in amazement. "So intelligent!"

"Yeah, she's a smartie," I said.

"You should see if she can catch a ball," Dad suggested.

"Do we have a ball?"

"A basketball," Dad said.

"We need a tennis ball. I'll add it to the shopping list." I tucked the leash under my armpit as I scribbled "tennis ball for dog" on the shopping list Mom keeps on the fridge. "I'm going to walk Bella down to Fuller Park. We'll be back in about an hour."

Dad nodded and started for the stairs. "Keep your

phone on," he said, very unnecessarily. I always have my phone on and charged.

Bella and I were halfway to the sidewalk when a blooping chirp informed me that someone wanted to video chat. I pressed the screen, and a moment later, my sister's face appeared. She had done something cool with her eyeliner. *Are her new friends into makeup?*

"Are you out with Bella?" Linden asked. I held the screen down to the dog and heard her coo, "She's beautiful! I can't believe you guys got a dog without me!"

"It happened really fast," I said, bringing the phone back up.

"I can't wait to meet her!"

"I know! June's so far away!"

"No, I'm planning on coming home next weekend!"

"You are?" My heart took off, like a kite on a windy day. "I can't wait to see you!"

"And I can't wait to meet the dog!"

Plunk. My metaphorical kite landed on the ground. "You're coming to see the dog?"

"I'm coming to see *everyone*," Linden said. "But I really want to meet Bella!" There was a noise behind her and Linden looked over her shoulder. "Yeah. Just a sec," she said, then turned back to me. "My roommate. I've got to go. But I'll see you soon! Bye, Bella! Bye!"

"Bye," I said, and clicked off.

Bella was looking up at me. "Apparently, my own sister wants to see you more than she wants to see me," I told her. A leaf caught Bella's attention, and she raced after it, sniffing it seriously once she had pinned it with her paw. I mean, I wasn't really that surprised. Linden has wanted a dog ever since her dwarf hamster, Arnold, died when she was in fourth grade.

Just be happy that she's coming home, I told myself. And, of course, there's nothing more guaranteed to make you happy than ordering yourself to do it.

The morning sky had been a clear, brilliant blue, but a line of gray clouds had appeared at the edge of the horizon and slowly marched in until they occupied the entire airspace. There's something about cloudy days in the spring—they make the budding leaves on the trees turn a foamy shade of green. It wasn't hot, but the air was damp, and the mud under my feet was soft and clingy as I walked. Bella's nose was to the ground as we made our way to the bike path that led into Fuller Park.

Fuller is the smaller of our town's two parks. It has walking paths and benches and a small pond at the center. Nunn Park, about a mile away, has mini golf, play structures, a splash pad, baseball diamonds, a train for kids, a petting zoo with sheep, and a concert space. When I was a kid, I used to say that Fuller Park and Nunn Park should switch names because Nunn Park was *fuller* of fun things, and Fuller Park had *none* of them. I still say that, to be honest. But both parks are named after the guys who founded them, so I guess they're not going to change.

I used to think Fuller Park was hideously lame—it didn't even have a swing set—but now that I'm older, I like to go for walks here sometimes. It's peaceful, and there's a frog that lives in the pond. I've named it Phyllis.

It was late afternoon, almost four, and there were a

bunch of older kids in the park. It's across from the high school, so sometimes they hang out there. A group of girls were throwing around a Frisbee, a small clump of band kids were using their instrument cases as pillows as they lay under a big tree, and a couple was having a very intense-looking conversation on a nearby bench. There was also an older woman with a little Pekingese mop of a dog that wagged eagerly as Bella approached.

"Oh, Bella, don't do that!" I said as she sniffed the other dog in a very inappropriate place.

The woman laughed. "That's just them saying hello. It's actually very polite dog behavior."

I wanted to say *Ew*, but I didn't, and I tried not to think about the germs that were probably now at the tip of my dog's nose. The dogs circled each other, and their leashes got tangled. I dropped Bella's leash to try to sort it out when I heard someone shout, "Is that Bella?" and a moment later, my dog was running across the park.

"Get your dog!" the older woman shouted. "Before he runs into the street!"

I didn't think it was the time to explain that my dog was a girl, so instead I just bolted after her.

"I got her, don't worry, I got her!" Ant shouted. He was the person she was running toward. But when he lunged toward her, she veered away, and a moment later she leaped into the air.

I'm not really sure why I screamed. I mean, looking back on it, it wasn't a screaming situation. But Bella had just leaped into the air and caught the high-school girls' Frisbee, and—I don't know. The scream just came out of me.

Nobody else screamed, or even seemed to notice my scream. In fact, the high school girls all immediately clustered around Bella, who dropped the Frisbee and sat with a happy, smug look on her face. All the girls were petting and congratulating Bella for being such an amazing dog as Ant and I ran over. Ant—being an athlete—got there quicker than I did, and I was huffing and puffing. "Tha—tha—thanks for—could you just—?" I gestured toward the leash.

Ant grabbed it, and Bella turned toward him, tail wagging.

"She's so pretty!" one of the girls said, and snapped a photo of Bella on her phone.

"I love her!" said another.

"How did you teach her to catch Frisbees?" asked the third.

"I had no idea she could catch a Frisbee," I admitted.

For some reason, this made everyone say, "Awww!" And the tallest one grabbed the Frisbee and said, "Let's see if she'll do it again!" She turned to Ant. "Okay?"

"Let's do it!" he said, and unhooked the leash. The Frisbee was in the air before I could say, "No, wait!" and Bella tore across the grass after it.

"Oh no, I threw it too far!" the high schooler said, but Bella was like a streak of black-and-white lightning. She leaped forward and snatched the disc out of the sky. Everyone in the park exploded with cheers. Half of them had caught the moment on their phones.

"Bella!" I called. I could hear the fear in my own voice, but luckily she trotted back to me with the disc in her mouth. She dropped it at my feet and then sat, as if she were expecting a treat. "I'll have to owe you," I said, grabbing her collar. *You're not getting away from me again*, I thought, shuddering at the mental image my brain had helpfully supplied, of her running into traffic.

Ant handed me the leash as the Frisbee girls begged me to let her catch another. I could feel my face burning. I wanted to get out of there desperately, but I was afraid to speak—I was sure my voice would be quavering. Ant looked at me for a moment, then said, "Hey, I think we've got to head out. We've got that thing, right?"

I just stared at him.

Ant cocked his head. "You know—at your house?"

"Yes," I said quickly. "Yes, the . . . thing."

"See you later!" Ant called, and the high schoolers all said goodbye, although I think they were mostly talking to Bella, as Ant and I headed back in the direction of my house.

"Was that okay?" Ant asked. "I thought maybe you didn't want to stay."

"Yeah, thanks. I didn't. I just . . . I've only had Bella

a couple of days. I'm afraid she might run off, or something."

"That makes sense."

"It does?"

"Sure. She's really fast. If she ran off, you'd never catch her. Right, Bella?" Bella looked up at him and wagged.

"I feel kind of bad. It's hard to say no to people."

"They were all in high school. It's *impossible* to say no! So *awkward*, right?" Ant looked at me and smiled.

"*So* awkward," I agreed.

"You know, we should probably talk about the project."

"Yeah . . . I'm thinking we could do something about the *Epic of Gilgamesh*. A presentation on the story and maybe talk about cuneiform?" Cuneiform is the language that the Mesopotamians used for writing.

"Maybe we could do a creative take," Ant suggested. "Act part of it out or something. Of course, I'd be Gilgamesh. Oh, but maybe Harry has some ideas."

"When it comes to group projects, Harry isn't really the greatest."

"Well, Lizzie, maybe we don't have to be the greatest," Ant said. "I think it's more important to make an impression."

"It's important to get across the information."

"Maybe we can do both." Ant paused. "So, I actually live in the other direction." He grinned. "I guess we can skip that thing, right?"

"The fictional thing?" I said. "Yeah. Let's skip it."

"Bye, Bella," he said. Then he smiled at me again, shoved his hands in his pockets, and walked away. He had a smooth, casual way of walking. Most guys in middle school kind of slump around, but Ant walked with . . . I don't know. Style, almost.

And then I realized that it was weird to analyze someone's walk, so I turned to my dog and said, "Let's go home," and she tugged at the leash in the absolute right direction, and I started to wonder if maybe my dog was smarter than I was.

CHAPTER FIVE

Hippopotomonstrosesquippedaliophobia —
fear of long words

Whoever came up with this is just mean.

A few days later, Mom was sitting on the couch, still wearing her pajamas and drinking coffee when Bella and I came downstairs. "Oh! Lizzie—and Bella—I have a surprise for you." Mom was making that special goofy smile she does when she has a secret. My mom is basically the world's worst secret keeper. Or at least happy secrets. If you tell her something personal or sad, she won't tell anyone. But she once made reservations for Disney World six months in advance and swore my dad to secrecy because she wanted it to be a surprise, and then she managed to not tell me and Linden for—I'm not kidding—forty-five minutes.

"What's up?" I asked.

Mom reached behind the couch and pulled out a large blue-and-purple-striped gift bag stuffed with pink tissue paper.

"Is this a harness?" I asked as I reached inside.

Mom put her hands over her mouth as if she might let out a little squeal.

Digging through the paper, I came out with a pink harness. Across the side was a patch that read EMOTIONAL SUPPORT in all capital letters.

"Now you can take Bella to school with you!" Mom said.

"I . . . what? Doesn't she have to be certified, or something?" I had never seen an emotional support dog in my school.

"She is certified! Look in the bag!"

I dug around and came up with an official-looking letter. "How did you . . ."

"There's a website that does it! Isn't that great?"

I mean . . . is it great? I wondered. *Do I even want Bella at school with me? Then I'll be the Girl with the Dog, and I'll probably have to talk to people all day.*

Then again, Bella is so sweet. I imagined having her sleep at my feet while I was at my desk. That *did* sound relaxing. "Does it . . . have to say 'emotional support' on the harness?"

"Oh, no, that comes right off." Mom reached for the patch and tore it away with a ripping Velcro noise. "Service dogs don't need to wear anything that says they're a service dog."

"But . . . she's not a service dog."

"She's an emotional support dog," Mom said.

I winced. "I mean, is she *really*?"

Narrowing her eyes, Mom pointed to the paper and said, "Believe it." Then she smashed the EMOTIONAL SUPPORT patch back into place on the harness. "Let's see how it fits." She called to Bella, who sat patiently while Mom figured out how to adjust the harness. Then she stood back and said, "Looks good."

"She's really cute in pink," I said, while thinking, *I am taking that patch off when we leave this house.*

"There's a matching leash at the bottom of the bag."

I could feel a nervous twinge in my stomach, but just then we heard a car door slam and steps at the side door.

"Knock, knock!" Mimi called, coming inside with the silver serving platter. "Thank you for letting me use this; just thought I'd drop it off on my way to the dentist! Oh, look, you're both still in your pajamas."

"We don't have to leave for school for another half hour," I explained.

Mom took the platter and said, "You're welcome to borrow it anytime."

Mimi smiled brightly. "I'm glad *someone* is getting some use out of it! It was very expensive, you know. Well, I'll get out of your hair!" She turned to leave, but when she saw Bella, she stopped in her tracks. "What's this?"

Mom straightened up. "Bella is our new registered emotional support animal. She's going to school with Lizzie."

Mimi rolled her eyes. "Emotional support for what?"

"Lizzie has been dealing with a lot of anxiety," Mom explained while I contemplated hiding behind the drapes.

"She's in middle school," my grandmother snapped. "What does she have to be anxious about?" She looked at me, shook her head, and I thought that it had clearly been a very long time since *she* was in middle school because there is a *lot* to be stressed about there. "Are you going to go through life taking a dog everywhere?"

This irked me. True, I wasn't sure I wanted Bella to come to school with me. But I didn't appreciate Mimi being so rude about it. Lots of people really need their dogs! "Blind people do it," I pointed out.

Mimi let out a loud "HA!" and then said, "You're hardly *blind*. But I guess everyone has a diagnosis these days. Which reminds me! How is Linden?"

I wanted to scream, but my mother was very polite and managed to use her cheerful voice to say, "Oh, very well! We just got her progress report. All As!"

"You received a progress report?" Mimi blinked her long-mascaraed lashes. "Shouldn't I have received a copy? After all, I am paying for this so-called school."

The vein in my mother's forehead looked like it was about to pop out, but luckily Dad walked in on this last comment. "Hi, Mother," he said, his voice perfectly even.

"Did you see this?" Mimi gestured toward Bella, still in her harness, who had hopped onto the couch.

As far as I knew, Dad had no clue about the emotional support registration thing, but he did know how to handle his mother. "Yes, isn't it wonderful?" he said. "Let me walk you out to your car." And then he managed to wrangle her out the door in the nicest possible way, listening patiently while my grandmother told him all about how nice it was to have a silver platter, even though *some* people don't appreciate it.

Mom waited until the door was shut before she muttered, "Well, it's not really any of your business, Mimi." Then she looked at me, this gleam in her eye. "We're taking Bella to school," she announced.

"Wait, today?" I called as Mom stormed upstairs. "I'm pretty sure we have to get permission!" Mom didn't reply. "Uh, okay," I said a half second before she slammed her bedroom door. Then I sighed and walked over to Bella. I stroked her soft head, hoping it would ease the nausea that continued to build in my stomach. "It'll be okay," I whispered, but Bella didn't seem convinced, and—to tell you the truth—neither was I.

I felt too sick to eat breakfast, so I just let Bella into the yard, fed her, and then went upstairs to get dressed. It was slow going: Dread had made my fingers feel weirdly numb.

Bella seemed to sense my feelings. She sat on the end of my bed, watching me. "Are you going to be my emotional support through *this*?" I asked. "Because I'm going to need it."

I was dragging my feet, hoping we would be late and

arrive after the bell rang, but Mom was stomping around, getting ready in the loudest way possible. My grandmother has the power to put my mother in an absolutely terrible mood, and my mom in a terrible mood is a very scary thing. It doesn't happen a lot, but when it does, watch out. So when she popped her head into my room and said, "We have three minutes and I expect you to be in the car on time," in that particular tone she has, I realized that my delay tactics might get me out of the frying pan and straight into the fire.

We got into the car without speaking, and I popped an earbud into my right ear. There's a Taylor Swift song, "Cowboy Like Me," that usually manages to calm me down. It wasn't really doing anything this morning, though. Bella was in the back seat, watching eagerly out the window. I pulled out my phone and texted Monique.

> **Mom on a mission and we are bringing bella to school as support dog tell me its going to be okay**

I only had to wait a moment before Monique's text popped up.

OMG that's great! Will be so cool!

But I still felt weird as we pulled up. Mom navigated the crowded parking lot and parked.

I watched as students pulled up on bikes or spilled out of bright orange-yellow buses. Everyone was walking in clumps toward the front doors. "Mom, are you sure this is a good idea?" I asked. "I mean, we haven't asked permission—"

Mom stared at the school. "Never ask permission. Only ask forgiveness."

"Did you, like, read that on a mug or something?" I asked. "Because I'm not sure—" Mom yanked open her car door and stepped out. "Okay, I guess we're doing this." She took Bella's leash and we headed for the front doors. "Am I just walking in, or—"

"Just walk right in," Mom said. "I'm here if anyone says anything."

"Maybe I should hold the leash?"

Mom handed it over. Bella was super excited as we made our way to the front doors. She was wagging and alert, and we got a lot of *aww!* reactions. "Oh no," I muttered as one kid started filming.

We'd made it three steps into the building when Vice Principal Walker stepped in front of us. She's always positioned at the front doors before first bell to "greet" everyone as we come in (that is, make us spit out our gum and put away our phones). She was smiling, but she also had her huge walkie-talkie out and ready. "I'm sorry, pets aren't allowed in the building," she said.

I scanned the hallway. Already a few kids were gathering to look at Bella. Beyond them, I finally spotted Monique. She gave me an excited smile and wave, but she hung back. Nobody really wants to bust in on a conversation with the vice principal. When she saw Monique, Bella pulled at the leash a little.

"This isn't a pet," my mother said confidently. "This is a service animal."

Ms. Walker sighed. Mom was already somewhat famous at school after the three years she had spent offering the administration "constructive criticism" about how to work with Linden. "What task has this dog been trained to perform?" the vice principal asked.

"You can't legally ask me that question."

"That is one question that I *can* legally ask, and I'm asking it, Francie." I think it's important to note that Vice Principal Walker has worked in this middle school for over twenty years.

"Fine. She has been trained to offer emotional support."

The vice principal looked down at my dog, who was pacing, eagerly looking at students and trying to sniff backpacks as people walked past. Ms. Walker sighed. "This isn't a service dog, but even if it were, the administration would have to have a meeting about how to proceed so that the animal causes the least amount of disruption to the students. And we can always refuse if Lizzie isn't in control of her dog."

"Lizzie will absolutely keep Bella under control at all times."

"She doesn't even have her under control *now*," Ms. Walker said as a passing student stooped to pet Bella, and Bella jumped on him, knocking the breakfast muffin sandwich from his hand and onto the floor.

"Bella, no!" I shouted as she scarfed it down. I tried to pry her jaws open, but she wouldn't budge. I managed to rip half an English muffin from her mouth and I flung it across the hallway, but Bella lunged after it. Spotting something on the floor, she gobbled that up before I could stop her or even see what it was.

"I think that was an eraser!" said the person whose breakfast my dog had stolen. My stomach swooped—it was Rex Heartson. "My sandwich is over there!" Monsoon season was starting in my armpit area, and I felt my throat growing tight. I struggled to breathe.

"Are you okay?" Mom asked.

"I'm fine," I wheezed.

"Here!" Mom reached for the plastic bone on Bella's leash. "Breathe into this poop bag!"

I pushed her hand away, hoping that Rex hadn't heard

that, and Ms. Walker watched without comment as I tried to get Bella to stop licking Rex. He was laughing, holding his hands up in mock surrender as she snuffled his hands, trying to find more breakfast sandwich.

Slowly, Ms. Walker turned her gaze to my mother. "I think we're done here."

"I don't think that dog is done," laughed Jeremy, Rex's best friend.

"Mom, please," I begged. My voice was thick and my nose was starting to run—I was about to cry. "Please take Bella home." I could see my dreams of becoming class secretary blowing away on the wind like a dusty tumbleweed, taking Rex with them.

My mom isn't usually like this. She's not a stubborn person. But, like I said, when she's in a particular mood, she's hard to reason with.

She grabbed Bella's leash. "I'm going to speak with Principal Yeoh," she announced.

"Please do," Ms. Walker said. "He can confirm what I've told you."

Mom's jaw shifted, and I was worried that she was going to go even more Karen-y, but the bell (luckily) rang. "I've got to go," I said to my mom.

"Bye, honey," she called as I ducked down the hall, my eyes burning. The hallway blurred, and I kept my face pointed at my shoes so that the tear would fall straight to the floor and not drip all over my face.

Monique hurried after me, but I didn't slow down.

I had to get to the girls' room so that I could just be by myself in a quiet stall for a few minutes. Or possibly for the rest of my life.

"Let's get this party *started*," Ant said as he dropped into the chair across from mine. "Let's *crush* this project on planned communities in the Indus Valley or on the *Epic of Gilgamesh* or whatever we decide to do!"

I put my hands over my eyes. "I can't deal with this."

"What's up?" Ant turned to Harry, who shrugged.

"She's spinning out."

"What are you spinning out about?" Ant asked.

"I can't—I can't—" I truly felt like I was about to cry. I couldn't even talk about how all my dreams were circling the drain, and I'd probably be transferring to Greenwood Academy, only Linden would want to avoid me in front of her cool new friends, so I'd have to eat lunch by myself in the bell tower and I'd stop talking to anyone and lose my voice and—

"It's embarrassment related," Harry explained.

"Oh, is it about your dog and your mom and that breakfast sandwich thing?" Ant asked.

I dropped my hands from my face. "How did you even hear about it already?"

"I dunno, it was a dog in school—a lot of people thought she was cute, people were excited," Ant said. "Don't worry about it! Hey—would you like a poop bag to breathe into?"

With a groan, I put my hands back over my face.

"Look, Lizzie, if you're going to worry about anything,

worry about this project," Harry said. "It's our last chance to rescue our grade."

"Not helping, Harry. Besides, my dog ate an eraser! Now I'm afraid that she'll get sick." *And my dad is going to lose it when he hears this story*, I thought.

"Oh, are you guys talking about your dog?" April was passing out a written version of Ms. Dobbler's assignment. "I heard she basically attacked Rex."

"She didn't attack anyone," I said.

"Wow, that's not the way I heard it," April said. "My dog, Larry, has been really well trained. I'm so glad he's never done anything like that. I'd be so embarrassed." She gave me a little smile, then turned and said, "Hi, Ant," before sauntering off to the next group.

Ant turned back to me and dropped his voice to a whisper. "Look, dogs can get freaked out when they're in new places," he said. "You just need to take her out more. Let her interact with lots of people! Then you get her attention, and when she pays attention to you, you give her a treat. That way, she knows that being distracted is bad, and paying attention is good. I can show you sometime, if you want."

A good chunk of my brain was still occupied replaying my mother shouting, "Breathe into this poop bag!" so I couldn't quite grasp what Ant was suggesting. "You could show me?"

"Sure—I could meet you and Bella at the park, or something."

"We could just meet at your house," Harry suggested. "But I can't stay long or I'll get hives."

"What do you know about dogs?" I was seriously confused.

"Nothing. But we have to work on this project." Harry shrugged.

"Great idea!" Ant said. "We have to meet, anyway. We'll just meet at your house and I can show you how to train Bella. We could even teach her a few tricks!"

"Sounds good," Harry said just as Ms. Dobbler came up to us. She was wearing a charcoal gray turtleneck and light gray slacks—a very colorful outfit, for her. She blinked at us from behind her thick glasses and said, "How's it going over here?"

"Awesome! We're just making plans to meet up after school," Ant said. "We're going to Lizzie's house."

Dobbler nodded. "Excellent. Have you chosen your topic? Any questions for me?"

Ant and Harry looked at each other. "*Epic of Gilgamesh*," I said.

"We're set," Harry said.

She nodded and moved on to the next group.

"Okay, look, I don't want to talk about my dog anymore," I said. "I made this schedule for us." I tapped at my tablet screen and flipped it around so that they could see. "The green assignments are for Harry—I thought that you could put together the slides. Ant, you're purple. Your biggest job is to pick a scene from the epic and act it out or do a dramatic reading. I'm red."

Ant peered at the chart. "What's that?"

"Everything else. I'll talk about cuneiform, how the epic was written and performed, all that stuff."

"So when should we come over, Lizzie?" Ant asked. "This afternoon, maybe?"

"Oh, well, my sister is visiting—"

"Linden's coming home?" Harry looked delighted.

"Yeah, Dad is picking her up today." Greenwood is in Vermont, about three hours away by train, and then another thirty from the station. "But I think I'll have some time in the afternoon on Saturday or Sunday."

"Saturday's no good," Harry said.

"So—Sunday? Like three?" Ant suggested.

I heard myself say, "Sure," and the plan was made. And then an image of Bella doing a running leap to smash into Rex and knocking him onto his butt popped into my mind and I actually cringed. Ant said, "Are you okay?" and then I cringed even more.

"She's imagining a worst-case scenario," Harry explained. "Like, making up a story in her head about how now that her dog ate a breakfast sandwich, everyone's going to hate her and we'll all start an underground newspaper about how dorky she is."

"Is that true?" Ant asked.

I nodded. "Kind of."

"Hm." Ant pointed to my head. "Your brain sounds like a dangerous weapon."

"It can be," I admitted.

He blew a breath toward his bangs, and they lifted slightly. His scar appeared for a half second, then disappeared behind a scrim of brown hair. "Then let's use it for good."

CHAPTER SIX

Nostophobia—fear of returning home

This would be seriously terrible. I guess I'm just glad that Linden doesn't have it. Wait—what if Linden gets it? That would be horrible! What if she decides she never wants to come home again? What if she only wants to meet me at Greenwood or at a doughnut shop, or something?

I'm starting to wonder if it's a good idea to be looking up these phobias.

I walked into the house to find Dad, Mimi, and Linden in the living room. Bella was at Linden's feet, and when they saw me, they both jumped up to give me a hug. Bella was wagging so hard that her rear end was wiggling all over the place, and Linden was so excited that she was bouncing up and down. After the day at school that I'd had, all their joy felt like diving into a cool swimming pool.

Linden squeezed me into a hug and I squeezed back. I was so happy to see her, but I couldn't help noticing that she smelled different. New perfume? New detergent? Whatever it was, it was nice, kind of flowery and talcum-powdery, but it didn't smell like Normal Linden smell. The hug ended and she grabbed my hands, smiled at me, and said, "What's wrong?" I felt my eyes fill with tears.

I bent down to pet Bella and said, "Nothing."

"Your sister's got anxiety, apparently," Mimi announced.

"Mom." Dad shook his head.

"What?" Mimi demanded. "That's what the dog is for, I thought."

"Well, she'll be cured now that I'm home," Linden said. Taking my hand, she pulled me to the couch, where she tucked herself into her favorite corner. "I already have plans for us. There's that new mystery movie—I thought we could check that out. And we have to get some bagels from Bagel Town—I've been craving them so much! I want to do all the things I've been missing while I've been at school! We spent all of spring break in Mexico, and I've missed out on all of the homeyness."

"Are you kidding?" Mimi asked. "That school has everything." I glanced over at Dad, who gave me a lifted-eyebrow smile.

"What's that look all about?" Linden asked.

"Dad's unhappy with Fuller and thinks maybe I should go to Greenwood," I explained.

"Really?" Linden grabbed my hand. "That would be so great! I miss you so much!"

"You do?" Her bright smile made me feel as if all the negative feelings of the past few days were burning off, like fog in sunshine.

"Of course I do! I miss everything about being home," Linden pointed out.

Mimi cast a doubtful eye around our shabby living room. "I'm not sure why."

Following her glance, I noticed some small paper cards taped to the wall near the light fixture. "What's that?" I asked.

"Oh, just some paint samples." Mimi waved a hand dismissively. "I brought them for your mother to look at—it's really time to freshen up this place."

"That's nice of you, Mom," Dad said as Linden and I exchanged a sideways look. Our mom was *not* going to appreciate hearing that our house needed to be freshened up. After the whole scene this morning, I thought she'd probably rather burn the place down.

"Linden was just telling us about school," Dad prompted.

"Oh, right! So we're doing a play, and I was thinking of auditioning, but I really don't have enough time because of basketball."

"What's the play?" Dad asked.

"Something called *The Crucible*?"

"About the Puritans?" Mimi asked. "By Arthur Miller?"

Linden shrugged. "I guess. It's definitely about Puritans."

Mimi looked impressed. "That's a very difficult play."

"Most of the parts go to older students. Our theater teacher—he's directing it—everyone says he's really good. And one girl in our school was even in a show on Broadway. She's a senior, though."

Mimi nodded. "Oh, so there are normal kids at the school, too?"

I felt like something had passed through me—a ghost or something—taking my spirit and just leaving a cold emptiness at the center of my body. Linden looked like someone had slapped her.

"Mom, there are all kinds of kids there," Dad said.

"I thought it was a special school," Mimi said.

I didn't know what to say. I just watched my sister as something seemed to click into place in her mind. Her expression changed, and she smiled. "It is a special school. They have a lot of resources, Mimi," she said. "It's great."

"Well, I'm glad to hear that," Mimi said. "So, see, Lizzie? You don't even have to have anxiety to go there."

I'm hardly ever speechless, but I was at that moment.

But I didn't have to say anything, because Linden managed to continue talking, as if everything was fine and Mimi wasn't being a horrible person, and we lived in a normal family where fathers stood up for their daughters and grandmothers were nice.

Our three-season porch has a roof that's nearly flat. It's on the same side of the house as Linden's room, and sometimes we crawl through her window and sit out there, looking up at the sky. That's where I found her after dinner. Her phone was in her lap, face down, and the fluffy gray blanket that usually sat at the foot of her bed was wrapped around her shoulders. Overhead, the almost-full moon wore a fuzzy halo beside a gray cloud.

"Knock, knock," I said gently from the window.

"Oh," Linden twisted her head so that she could smile at me. "There you are."

"Okay if I join you?"

"I've been waiting." She lifted her arm, draped in the blanket, like a furry wing. I settled beside her, pulling the edge of the blanket over me.

"Were you texting someone?" I asked, nodding at the phone.

"Thinking about it. But I don't think anyone would really get what Mimi's like, you know?"

I mashed my lips together for a moment. "I wasn't even sure if it bothered you," I said.

"*Special school.*" She rolled her eyes.

"Well, it *is* special," I admitted. "They have a stable full of horses and a bell tower from 1753."

"I'm so glad you were paying attention on the tour. But we both know that's not what Mimi meant. She thinks I'm defective."

I sighed. "You and me both. 'Lizzie,'" I mimicked, "'you don't even have to have anxiety to go there!' She makes it sound like Mom and Dad sent you away to an institution, not a fancy private school."

"You know what really makes the place special?" Linden said. "The classes are really small, like eight kids in each, and my teachers understand my situation. I can just concentrate on doing the work. I don't feel like someone with a diagnosis and an IEP. I just feel like a regular student."

"There are thirty people in my social studies class," I said. "This one guy, Ant, has to sit on a stool."

"Firework Guy?"

"Yeah." I realized that the nickname suddenly bothered me. "He's not that bad, actually."

"Interesting." My sister leaned back on her elbows.

"What's interesting?"

"It's just—you always told me that you didn't trust him. That he had terrible judgment, and that you were going to stay far away from him."

"I did? Well, I didn't even know him back then."

"Interesting."

"Stop saying that!" I gave Linden a playful push, and she laughed.

"I don't mean anything weird; it seems good! I'm glad you're giving someone a chance, Lizzie. You often see people in black and white. Good or bad. Safe or scary."

"Most people *are* scary, because most people only care about themselves."

Linden tucked a lock of her long brown hair behind her ear and adjusted the blanket, which had partially fallen from her shoulder. "Do you really believe that?"

"You don't?"

She seemed to think it over. "I guess I think most people don't mean any harm. They may hurt your feelings or do the wrong thing, but it's usually because they don't know any better."

"Like Mimi? She's like seventy years old—you don't think she knows better?"

"I mean, as a grandmother, she's not going to be starring in a homestyle bakery commercial. She's pretty vain and she can be rude and spiteful . . . but I don't know. She is paying for half of my tuition at the 'special school.'"

I snuggled closer to Linden. "She's always so rude about it."

"I know. But I feel like that's because . . . I don't know. Maybe she's just trying to remind everyone that she's doing something nice."

"Normal people don't do that."

"It's insecurity, you know? She's just saying, 'Love me.' It makes me wonder what her life has been like."

I can honestly say that I had never in my life for even a split millisecond wondered what my grandmother's life had been like. I really didn't know much about her past, except that my grandfather had been a successful surgeon at the biggest hospital in the region. They met in medical school, but Mimi dropped out to get married and raise my dad and his brother. Did she miss my grandfather? Did she regret giving up on her career? Was she lonely? I'd never wondered, but Linden clearly had. My sister had trouble with instructions and reading, but she could read people. She *understood* them.

I put my head on her shoulder. Her hair was damp. She must have used the shampoo she left here, because she smelled like the old Linden again.

"You really are special," I told her.

"Thanks," she said.

"But not in the Mimi way."

She laughed so hard that she fell over sideways, and then I started laughing, and then neither of us could stop. In the light of the streetlamp, an elderly couple out for an evening stroll with their tiny chihuahua looked around, trying to discover where the cackling was coming from. "Up here!" Linden called, and when they saw us on the porch roof, they laughed, and we laughed more, until it seemed like the neighborhood was filled with the sound of our voices, loud enough to reach the fuzzy moon in the sky.

It was Sunday afternoon, and Monique was over. It was back to being sweater weather, and we had decided to make some strawberry muffins, which made the whole house smell wonderful, like vanilla and berries. Linden was out with her best friend, Sascha, and Mom was playing in her soccer-for-old-people club. Dad was upstairs, rearranging a closet. That's the kind of thing he likes to do on Sundays. Bella was asleep on the couch. Nice life.

"You don't think they're ready yet?" Monique asked, opening the oven for the fifteenth time.

Gently, I pushed the oven door closed. "They need another six minutes."

Pursing her lips, Monique reached for the box of mix. "Not according to these instructions."

"Trust me; I've made these before. Six more minutes."

She flung herself dramatically onto a kitchen chair. "Okay, fine. But I can take a few home, right? You don't need them all for the group?"

"The group is just me, Harry, and Ant."

"Well, Harry will eat three," Monique said. "And Ant will probably have the rest."

"Harry and Ant can each have *one*," I said. "Or none.

Whatever. I was hoping to have one for Linden and one for each of my parents."

"And one for you."

"I deserve two. But that means . . ." I did a little mental math. "That means you can take five."

"Oh, perfect! One for me now, then one each for me, Mom, Darius, and Andre later." Monique has two older brothers in high school who are both extremely nice. Darius is shy and really into music. He's the drum major in the marching band, and Monique has been trying to give him lessons in how to be more assertive (which basically means teaching him to yell at people), but apparently he's not really very receptive to the coaching. Andre is a freshman who made it onto the varsity soccer team. He's super popular; some senior girl apparently asked him to the homecoming dance, which was a big deal since Monique's mom didn't want him out past nine. It's so funny how people can grow up in the same family and have the same genes and somehow be incredibly different. Like Linden and me. She's good with people, and she's sweet and confident, and I'm just . . . I don't know, worried and awkward.

"Okay, listen, can we just talk about the campaign for one more minute?" Monique asked. "Because I'm about to launch."

"Uggghh."

"I'm hearing *yes*. I'll put up and send out the flyers tomorrow, but . . ." She held out her phone to show me the design. I liked it. It was simple. April's posters had a picture of her surrounded by rainbows and sparkles, but I wasn't into that. "I think our slogan could be punchier."

"What's wrong with Vote for Lizzie?"

Monique grimaced and took a prim sip from her water glass.

"Okay, it's pretty basic," I admitted. "I don't know. I'm not good at this stuff! I just want to plan fundraisers!"

"How about, I Just Want to Plan Fundraisers," Monique suggested.

"I guess I'd rather be too basic than too *weird*."

Monique held up her phone. On the screen was a virtual

flyer that read APRIL FOR SECRETARY. AT LEAST SHE HAS COOL IDEAS! The photo was April with a cupcake.

"What is that?" I asked. "What's that supposed to mean?"

"It's on Martin Mayer's story—he reposted it," Monique said. "I think April's implying that she's going to do bake sales and that you aren't good at coming up with ideas."

"Well, that is rude. Martin Mayer is a jerk, and I wouldn't want him voting for me, anyway."

"Do you understand how voting works?" Monique demanded. "There are a *lot* of jerks in our class, and we *need* them to vote for you."

"Let April have the jerks," I said. But my eyes were stinging. April didn't have to say "at least" like that! Did people think I couldn't come up with good ideas? But even if I didn't—so rude!

My phone notification dinged. It was Harry. "Can't make it to group today," I read aloud. *"What?"*

Monique flicked her fingers at me. "Call him."

130

So I did. "What the heck, Harry?"

His voice was tinny over the speakerphone. "I made the next round."

"What? What next round?"

"The *Zombiesquad* tournament," he explained. "I made it through the first round, the one where they let regular gamers compete. Next round is against pros. And it's in seven minutes!"

"Oh my gosh, Harry, that's amazing!" Monique said.

"Ugh . . ." I rolled my eyes. "That is amazing," I admitted.

"I'll make it up to you," Harry said.

"You better," I said. "And good luck."

"Yeah, good luck!" Monique chirped as the timer went off. "Muffins!"

"He is *not* getting one," I grumbled as Monique put on the oven mitts and pulled the muffins out of the oven. They were beautifully toasted on top. "Perfect!" I said, and at that moment, someone knocked on the side door.

I could see through the window that it was Ant, waving.

His voice was muffled as he called, "What smells so amazing? I can smell it from out here."

I waved him in, and he spotted the muffins on the counter. "Did you make those for the group?" he asked. "I hope?"

"I mean . . . we made them," I said. "And you can have one."

"Hello, hello, hello!" Ant said as Bella trotted into the kitchen. She'd heard the door. When she spotted Ant, she galloped up to him, and he rubbed her sides. "Who's the best dog? Who's the bestest dog?"

"Oh, by the way, Harry can't make it," I said.

"So we get Monique instead?"

"I wish," Monique said. "My group is extremely boring. Listen, I'll get out of the way. Just let me take a few of these."

I got out a plastic container and put the warm muffins inside. "Let them cool off before you put on the lid," I said. "Or else they'll get soggy."

Monique plucked an extra muffin from the tray. "I'm taking this to Harry."

"Wait, he's not sick?" Ant asked.

"No," I said. "He's just made it into the next round of his zombie *pew-pew!* tournament."

"You're kidding!" Ant looked deeply impressed. "That's a really big deal. Well, maybe Bella can join our group!"

Monique took off. Ant and I each took a muffin and got settled at the kitchen table. Bella curled up at our feet as we got to work.

It was kind of fun, actually. Ant had a great idea for the poster—we'd do it like an action movie—and we brainstormed most of the slide presentation. "I know Harry doesn't love doing oral presentations. And I don't, either," I admitted.

"Well, we all have to do a bit of the oral presentation," Ant said. "But I love that stuff. I'll do most of it."

"We already have a lot of information on the slides," I said. "I think Harry can just get the images and write captions."

Someone fumbled at the door, and Mom walked in with Linden. Mom was still sweaty from her soccer game, but her cheeks were pink and she was smiling. "Oh, hi!" she said when she saw Ant. "I thought Monique was over." She lifted her eyebrows and blinked at me in a way that I did not love as Bella got up to demand attention and pets.

I introduced my mother and Linden to Ant. "We're working on a social studies project," I explained. "Harry's supposed to be here, too, but he couldn't make it."

"I'm going to go put this away," Linden said, indicating the shopping bags she was carrying. "Nice meeting you, Ant."

"So!" Mom said brightly as she washed her hands. "Antonio, can I offer you anything? Would you like some sparkling water? Regular water?"

"I can get it myself," Ant said. "If you just show me where the glasses are."

Mom got a glass from the cupboard and handed it to him. Then, when he was busy at the sink, she turned to face me and mouthed, *He's cute!*

I glared at her and shook my head.

"Ice?" Mom asked.

"This is fine," Ant said, taking a sip. Bella went to her toy box and pulled out a fabric Frisbee. Then she walked to Ant and looked up at him. "Oh, you want to play? You want to catch the Frisbee?" He looked over at me. "Think we can take a little break?"

"You should definitely take a break!" Mom said, although no one had asked her. And then she *winked* at me. I wanted to strangle her.

"Let's go in the yard," I suggested, mostly so that we could get away from my mom's smiles and winks. Why do parents have to make everything weird?

Our yard isn't anything special. It's mostly just flat green grass with two dead potted plants in the corner. But it's a good size, so when Ant tossed the Frisbee, Bella had room to race after it. She brought it back, and he tossed it again.

"Would it be okay with you if I tried to teach her a trick now?" Ant asked. "Have you got a few dog treats?"

I went inside and grabbed the bag. Bella was watching me very carefully. As I handed it over, Ant asked, "Does she know sit?"

Bella sat.

Ant laughed. "Awesome! I guess she does! Cool." I sat on the grass as he started to teach her how to shake. It was pretty interesting. First, he said, "Shake," as he tickled the back of her right front leg, and when she moved it, he gave her a treat. Then he repeated the process a few times.

"She got this really fast," Ant said as he repeated, "shake," and Bella moved her foot, then stared at the treat bag. Next, he said, "Shake," and held out his palm. When she moved her paw, he placed his palm under her paw. A few more of those, and she was putting her paw on his palm the minute he said, "Shake."

"This is a smart dog."

"She is," I agreed.

"Do you mind recording this on my phone for me?" Ant asked. "I want to show my parents."

"Part of your secret dog-getting plan?"

"Devious minds think alike," he said. "I have to prove that I'm actually good at this. They have doubts."

So I recorded him doing shake with Bella. Then I

recorded him officially teaching her to fetch. She hadn't really mastered letting go of the Frisbee until Ant showed her what to do and rewarded her with a treat.

"I'm learning a lot," I said as I took a video of Bella racing after the Frisbee. "I don't have a lot of dog experience."

"There are tons of great videos," Ant said. "I'll send you some links."

Bella came over to me and dropped the Frisbee at my feet. "Good girl," I said, patting her on the back. *She really is a great dog*, I thought.

CHAPTER SEVEN

Kakorrhaphiophobia—fear of failure

Everyone has this...right? I mean, everyone fears that they will get precisely one vote for class secretary (their own) and that this will open the floodgates to people mocking them nonstop. Lots of people worry that losing an election for class secretary will be the start of a downward spiral that ruins their self-esteem, friendships, and grades, right?

The minute Mom dropped me off at school the next

morning, an extremely popular eighth grader named Sophie Waller did something very weird. She looked me right in the eye and said, "Hi! Vote for Lizzie!" And then all of her friends giggled.

I felt my cheeks burning, and I mumbled, "Hi," while my mind completely spun out. *How does Sophie know my name? And why did she say hi to me? She can't even vote for next year's eighth-grade officers—what does it mean?* And while I was lost in those thoughts, Johnny Ramirez-Figueroa was like, "Yo, vote for Lizzie!" and then his friends Simon and Xavier were like, "Hey, go, Lizzie!" and I realized that something truly horrible was going on.

Not surprisingly, I started to feel nauseated. I worried that the toaster waffle I'd eaten for breakfast was going to sneak up my throat, but I put my head down and headed into the school. My chest felt tight; I could hardly breathe. Everyone was making fun of me. Had I accidentally become famous for almost breathing into a poop bag? It's not like there was poop in it!

My underarms were suddenly damp with sweat, and that

freaked me out even more. I needed to hide, but it felt impossible. A cluster of eighth-grade boys watched as I walked past them in the hallway, the artsy crowd waved at me from their spot on the floor near the teacher's lounge, and then the band teacher, Mr. Wilson, said, "Well, well, hello there."

I'm not even in band!

I ignored him, turned on my heel to head to the nurse's office, and nearly ran over Monique. "Lizzie! You're a celebrity!" she said, shoving a phone into my face. I took it from her, but I could hardly hold it straight—my hands were shaking too badly.

"What's going on?" I asked as I watched a video play.

It was Ant's face speaking into the camera. "Hey, Lizzie—watch this!" he said, and flipped it around to show me tossing a Frisbee. Bella raced after it, doing a twist in the air as she caught it. Then she raced up to the camera, dropped the disc, and looked up at the lens with big eyes. "Good dog!" said Ant's voice, and his hand came in from the side of the frame to hand her a treat, which she gobbled with a huge grin on her face. Then he panned over to me, smiling and clapping.

"How did you—"

"Ant posted it on Picbomb!" Monique said as the video automatically began to replay. "Then DogScores reposted it with eleven out of ten wishbones."

"I went . . . viral?"

"Just, like, mini-viral," Monique corrected. "And I think it's really Bella who went viral. But because DogScores is pretty popular and you're at our school, everyone's been sharing it."

"I'm not even on Picbomb!"

Monique grimaced guiltily.

"I'm on Picbomb?" I asked.

She scrunched up her face as if she was afraid I might get all up in it. "I made a profile for the campaign. Ant tagged it with the hashtag 'VoteforLizzie' . . . and so did DogScores."

"Oh my—"

"Uh, hey, Monique. Hey, both of you."

My mouth fell open and I froze.

"Oh, hey, Rex!" Monique said, putting on her most cheerful face. "What's up?" She gave me a not very subtle kick.

"Hello, how are you, hi, how are you, did I say that already, ha ha, that's funny, so what's new?" I said, and Monique kicked me again so I'd stop.

Rex smiled. "I'm good, but I wanted to talk to you. Ant invited me to come over to your place after school today, but I know that Ant is sometimes—" Rex waved his hands in an all-over-the-place gesture. "Is it cool?"

I gaped wordlessly. Would it be cool? For Rex to come to my house? TODAY?

"Oh, yeah, that's definitely okay—but let's do tomorrow instead," I did NOT say. Luckily, Monique said it.

Rex kept talking to me, as if I was the one who had replied. "That sounds good. He said around four thirty, if you're sure you don't mind? He wanted to show us how he's training your dog."

"Uh—uh—*us*?" I stammered, still trying to catch up to the conversation.

"Sounds amazing!" Monique said. "Bring friends! You have the address, right? See you tomorrow at four thirty!"

"Okay, cool!" Rex touched Monique on the shoulder as he passed by, and she gave him a wave as I managed to murmur, "Cool . . ."

Her head snapped to face me, her smile sending beams of light and energy. "This is amazing!"

"I think I'm going to throw up."

"No, you won't! This is huge! I'll come with you right after school tomorrow and put some snacks together while you, Ant, and Harry work on your project. You'll totally get your work done before people come over. Lizzie, do not look like that—this is *great* for your campaign!"

Oh, right. The campaign. I still felt shivery, and as if the floor was shifting beneath me. But the campaign . . .

"Lizzie! There you are!" Ant did that dramatic kind of jogging that people do when they want to show how hard they've been looking for you. "Listen, I might have invited a few people over to your house—"

"We heard." Monique rolled her eyes and folded her arms.

"It's fine. It's okay," I told him. "But next time, would you please check with me first?"

"I also posted a video with you in it," he confessed.

"We heard about that, too, dude," Monique said. She never says *dude*, and it sounded kind of threatening.

"I'm sorry. I swear I'm trying to be better. I get carried away sometimes!" His eyes were huge, reminding me of Bella. "Sorry, Lizzie. I can take the video down and tell people not to come—"

"No, it's fine," I said quickly. It wasn't really fine, but what could I say?

"It's cool, Ant," Monique added. "We told Rex he and his friends can come over tomorrow, not today, but next time—don't make plans without Lizzie."

"Okay!" He smiled brightly. "This is great! Thanks! Thank you!" Then he darted off down the hall.

"That guy." Monique shook her head.

"He's like a blender with the lid off," I said.

"I really think he means well," Monique said. "This whole thing is awesome. But he's a complete chaos agent."

As the bell rang, she added, "Which is, maybe, just what we need."

Linden and I were on the couch. Her feet were propped on her duffel bag, which was packed tight as a sausage with things she'd realized she couldn't live without at school. Dad was putting his shoes on so that he could drive her back to the train station.

"When can you visit next?" I asked.

"Term ends halfway through June," she said.

"That's like eight weeks from now."

"I know."

My phone dinged and I opened it to see a GIF of Bella fetching a Frisbee over and over. Yellow block letters screamed: VOTE LIZZIE! LET'S FETCH THOSE FUNDS!

Your new slogan! Monique texted.

"What's this?" Linden asked, leaning in to get a look. "Ohmigosh! So cute!"

"Is it weird, though?" I asked. "Like, does it make it look like people are voting for my dog?"

Linden rolled her eyes. "It says, 'Vote Lizzie.'"

"I know, but . . . it doesn't really say anything *about* me. Except that I have a cute dog."

Linden considered it. "I think you're overthinking this. It's just a funny slogan. You'll be the one who gets the votes, and you'll be the one who has to do the job. This is just a way of getting people's attention."

"I just feel kind of weird about it . . ."

"Do you want to tell Monique not to post it? Because she might have already put it up on socials—"

Right on cue, my phone buzzed with a call from Monique. She didn't even pause to say hello. "Oh my gosh, Ant already reposted your story and it's getting TONS of likes and reposts!" I hadn't heard Monique sound this excited since Bagel Town came out with a chocolate–peanut butter smoothie. "This is amazing—I told you his chaos might help us!

"And April's campaign has got, like, *nothing*. It's j—"

"Monique, I—"

"—ust a big hole where a campaign is supposed to go!"

Dad walked in, and Linden stood up. "Look, Monique," I said, "Linden is heading out—can we talk about this later?"

"No problem. I'm making more posts and flyers— Fetch Those Funds, The Choice Isn't Ruff, Nothing's Impawsible!—et cetera. Call me! Bye, Linden!" And she clicked off.

Smiling, Linden wrapped me in a warm hug.

"What am I going to do?" I murmured into her hair.

"Do?" Linden said with a laugh. "I think you're going to win!"

"Yoo-hoo!" Mimi called as she walked in—through our front door, for a change.

"Hm," Mom said quietly as she poked at the salad greens on her plate. "We should really keep that entrance locked."

We exchanged a smile over our turkey burgers, Mom's go-to meal when she can't deal with thinking of anything else to cook.

"Oh, hello, where is everyone?" Mimi pink-lipstick-frowned at me, then at Mom.

I tried not to roll my eyes. It's hard when your own grandmother doesn't seem to think of you as "someone."

"Gerald is driving Linden to the train station, then he's got a meeting downtown." Mom stood up to give Mimi a quick hug, but Mimi just air-kissed in Mom's general direction and then pouted.

"Linden left? Without saying goodbye?"

"She was in a rush to get back," I lied.

"Too much of a rush to say goodbye to her grand-mother?" Mimi lifted her carefully sculpted eyebrows. "This was really a drive-by visit, wasn't it?" She pulled out a dining chair and made a show of brushing invisible crumbs off the seat before sitting down.

I could practically hear my mom gritting her teeth as she asked, "Well, what brings you by?"

"Oh." Mimi shrugged. "I just wanted to get some of my paint samples back. I'm thinking of redoing the shed. Do you always let your dog into the dining room while you're having dinner?" She cast a disapproving glance at Bella, who was asleep on her dog bed in the corner.

"Is that bad?" I asked.

Mimi inspected her fingernails. "Is that how you like it?"

"How we like what?" Mom asked. "Having a dog?"

"Just . . . a dog, where you're eating." Mimi held up her hands, as if she was surrendering (which she was not). "If that's how you like it, it's fine. So, Lizzie, have you been taking Fido to school with you?"

"Do you mean Bella?" I asked.

"Sure, Bella. I can't get used to these human names for dogs!"

"Not yet," Mom said. "But I already spoke to Dr. Funk. And I've got a meeting set up with the principal first thing Friday morning."

"Am I coming to this?" I asked, startled.

"Yes, but you don't need to say anything." Mom stood up, and I handed her my nearly empty plate. She stacked it on top of her own and announced, "I'm just going to present the arguments in favor of having Bella come to school with you."

"Do I have to?" I called as Mom stepped into the kitchen.

Mom's voice floated out from the kitchen. "It's optional."

My grandmother's eyebrow arched, and she dropped her voice. "You know, sweetie . . ." Mimi leaned toward me. "You don't always have to go along with your mom's harebrained schemes. You don't have to drag that dog to school with you if you don't want to."

My cheeks burned with a mixture of embarrassment and anger as Mom reappeared, carrying a plate with chocolate-chip cookies and grapes. I couldn't tell if she'd overheard Mimi as she asked, "Would you like a little dessert?"

"Oh, I haven't had any dinner yet," Mimi said. There

was something about the tilt of her head that seemed to suggest that Mom should have offered to make her a turkey burger. Or maybe a prime rib. "I don't like to eat too many sweets, anyway." She gestured to her slim figure.

Just to let you know, my mom is not slim. She's soft and good for hugging, but I could tell that Mimi's comment bothered her, and I felt like I'd been stuck by an angry porcupine—little rage needles in my torso. "You know, Mom," I said suddenly, "I will come to that meeting with the principal." I picked up a cookie and smiled at Mimi. "I want Bella to come to school with me."

Mom smiled as she picked a grape off the stem and popped it into her mouth. "Sounds great, honey."

"Well," Mimi said, "I suppose I should leave you to it. I'm just going to pull those samples from the wall. I can see they're right by the front door, where I left them."

"Goodbye, Mimi," Mom said, and I waved.

We didn't laugh until she shut the door behind her.

The next day, Ms. Dobbler didn't give us time to work on our projects in class, which was very annoying because they were due Wednesday. Even with our plan to work after school, Harry, Ant, and I were behind.

"Oh, by the way, I have to leave early," Harry said as we walked to my house that afternoon with Ant and Monique.

I sighed, but I tried not to make it too dramatic. "More gaming?"

Harry nodded, and Ant punched him in the shoulder. "No way! You made it to the semifinals? That's amazing!"

Harry blushed and I felt my cheeks burn. *You could be nicer about Harry's hobbies*, I told myself. "That's . . . that is cool, Harry."

He smiled. "Don't worry, I'll get my part of the project done."

And that was that.

Harry and I started setting up our computers at the kitchen table while Monique washed her hands. After a minute, I noticed Ant wasn't at the table—because he was looking through our cabinets.

"What are you doing?" I asked him.

"Finding your snack stash," he replied, bending to reach into a deep drawer where Mom keeps the pots and pans.

"Oh, forget it," I said, waving at the fruit bowl. "My mother believes in healthy foods."

"Really?" Ant stood up, brandishing a bag of Cheetos. "Then explain *this*!"

"Busted," Harry said, fingers clicking on his keyboard.

Ant held up his other hand—he'd also found a bag of Doritos. Where had those come from? "Can I eat these?" he asked.

"Go ahead," Monique said as he tore into the bag with his teeth.

"No!" I yelped. "What are you doing?"

"Getting out a bowl," Monique said, even though I wasn't talking to her. "For the Doritos."

"I'll get you a replacement bag," Ant promised as he shoved another chip into his mouth. "I'm forry, I'm juft ftarving."

"Couldn't you have waited? Monique is making cookies!"

"That's going to take a while," she pointed out.

I gave her the Murder Stare. Whose side was she on?

Monique held out the bowl and Ant poured in the Doritos. I watched the chips fall, wondering whose secret stash it was—my mom's or my dad's. Neither of them were going to be happy about this.

Ant brought the bowl to the table and pushed it toward me like a peace offering. I ignored it.

"Fourteen minutes until I have to take off," Harry said, checking his phone.

"Okay." I opened my computer and checked the chart I had made. "So, Harry, you're in charge of—"

"Hey—sorry," Monique interrupted, "but do you know where I can find a mixer?"

I dug the mixer out of the cabinet and went back to the table. The doorbell rang.

Ant jumped out of his chair. "That's probably Sabine and Giselle. They're always early. I'll get it." Lovestruck, Bella trotted after him.

"Do you have a metal spatula?" Monique asked. I

pointed to the right drawer, and then Ant walked back in with Sabine, Giselle, Rosa, and Em—all soccer girls. Sabine petted Bella, saying, "Hello, Lizzie!"

"Hi," I said, and Sabine looked up at me.

"Hi," she said, which was kind of weird. Giselle sniffed the air and asked, "What smells so amazing?" She went over to join Monique, and the doorbell rang again.

Ant hurried to answer it, and I noticed Harry was shoving his notebook into his backpack.

"Wait—what's happening?" I asked. My chest was feeling tight. "What are you doing?"

"Leaving."

"We haven't even started!"

"This clearly isn't happening right now." Harry looked at me closely and said, "Hey, Lizzie. It's okay. We'll get this done."

"But—"

Ant walked into the kitchen with Rex, Jeremy, Ari, and Samir, and now my kitchen was crammed with the jock crowd, who I barely knew; people were eating my parents' secret snacks; and Harry was leaving.

"Hey, Lizzie!" Jeremy held out a piece of chip and Bella jumped up to eat it.

"She's got my vote!" Rex announced.

Something was happening with my ears. They felt thick and rubbery, and I couldn't quite hear properly. "Sorry," I said, and hurried to the bathroom. Locking the door, I closed the lid to the toilet and sat down. I did the thing that Dr. Funk taught me—count to four while breathing in, count to four while breathing out. I did that ten times, which made me feel a little better, so I did another ten. Then someone knocked gently on the door.

"Someone's in here," I shouted.

"It's me." Harry's voice.

"Just a second," I said. Standing up, I looked at myself in the mirror: not great. I looked a little queasy, which I was. I splashed water onto my face and dried it off with a hand towel.

When I finally opened the door, Harry and I stood facing each other for a moment.

"I thought you had to go?" I said.

"In a sec. Everyone went outside," he said. "Ant is showing off Bella's tricks in your yard."

I nodded, and Harry put a hand on my shoulder.

"It's okay," he said. "You're okay."

"Harry—does everyone think that Bella's name is Lizzie?"

"What? No way! You're just nervous."

I nodded. Harry doesn't talk much, but he gets me. "I'll walk you out."

In the kitchen, we found Monique and Rex chatting as she slid cookies from a baking sheet onto a plate. He laughed at something she said, and my stomach felt like I had swallowed a bucket of slime. She startled when she saw me, then smiled. "Hey, you doing okay?"

"I . . ."

"Too many Doritos," Harry said. Then he walked out the side door just as my mother walked in carrying a grocery bag. "What's all this?" she asked, gesturing to the backyard. "Who are all of these people?" She sounded kind of amazed.

I explained the situation as well as I could. "Basically, those are Ant's friends," I told her.

"Ah," she said. "And I'm glad to see you found Dad's snack stash." She was positively beaming—I guess she couldn't wait to tell Dad that the plan for me to try new activities and make new friends was already paying off. "You're welcome to anything you find. And what did you make, Monique? Chocolate-chip cookies?"

They chatted as Mom and I put away the groceries, and a moment later, everyone trooped inside. Bella raced over to me, clearly excited.

"Hey, everyone," Ant shouted. "This is Lizzie's mom!"

The group chorused hello, and Monique passed around the plate of cookies as Mom said, "Hello, everyone!"

"We love your dog!" Sabine called.

"Thank you!" Mom beamed. "We're trying to get the school to allow her as an emotional support animal."

I. Nearly. Fainted.

"Oh, that's so cool!" Em stroked Bella's tail. "You're going to come hang out with us?" The other soccer girls cooed in agreement, and Ant said, "That would be amazing."

Monique offered me a cookie. "I'm going to strangle my mother," I whispered.

"Remember, it's all great for the campaign!" she whispered back.

"Monique! People really think they're going to vote for a *dog*!"

"What? No, they don't. Not everything is a worst-case scenario." Then she turned away, asking, "Cookies, anyone?"

I fought the urge to run to the bathroom again. Everyone was smiling, chatting, having a good time. Ant walked over to me and said, "Thanks so much, Lizzie. This really means a lot to me."

I forced myself to say, "No problem," like a normal person.

I was the only one who knew that I wasn't normal. I was more like a human egg, trying not to crack.

I reached down and touched Bella's head, feeling her

thick, soft fur beneath my fingertips. She licked my hand.

I concentrated on listening to Ant's story about trying to get Bella to give back the ball. He laughed, so I laughed.

Masquerading as a normal person. My only superpower.

CHAPTER EIGHT

Emetophobia—fear of vomiting

This is one phobia that I'm pretty sure I do have. But it seems pretty normal to me to be afraid of vomiting. After all, it is humiliating. And disgustingly smelly. Unfortunately, I feel like I'm going to vomit *a lot*. My fear of clowns is pretty easy to manage. All I have to do is avoid circuses, which isn't difficult. But vomiting? Could happen at any time.

"We're up another two hundred and thirty-six likes!"

Monique's voice trumpeted from my phone. "And fifty-two reposts for Fetch Those Funds!"

"That sounds like a lot," I said.

"Ant and all of his friends are making a huge difference," she said. "Having them over today was brilliant! Have you written your speech?"

"I'm working on it." That was half true. I was *trying* to work on it, but so far I'd only written two sentences. And not even the first two sentences—ones that belonged somewhere in the middle. Maybe. "Monique . . . seriously . . . do you think that people think Bella's name is Lizzie, and that she's running for class secretary?"

"That's just a typical Lizzie worst-case scenario. They couldn't think that." Monique seemed to mull this over. "Could they?"

"I really think they might."

"Okay, but hear me out—does it matter? I mean—do you want to win or not?"

"I don't want my *dog* to win, Monique!"

"Well, you're the one giving the speech," Monique

pointed out. "So it's going to be pretty clear that you're Lizzie, right? And besides . . ." But she didn't make another point. Instead, she narrowed her eyes and asked, "Is it possible to write the speech so that it isn't clear whether you're speaking for the dog or speaking for yourself?"

"Monique, no!"

"Okay, okay. Don't do that. That's a bad idea. Just . . . write it and send it to me when you're done," Monique said, then clicked off. I was starting to think that maybe she was more into this election than I was.

I looked back at my computer screen, watching the cursor blink. Blink. Blink. A heavy weight settled onto my chest. After I finished my speech (*if* I finished), I had more work to do on the social studies project. Which reminded me . . .

I pulled out my phone.

Don't forget! Harry: Three more images needed for slides 4 and 7, plus info about the artifacts. Please cite sources! Ant: Finish the timeline (edit explanation of missing tablets in Epic).

A moment later, a thumbs-up appeared from Ant.

Nothing from Harry. I sighed.

Plink.

Something had landed against my window. When I looked out, I saw Harry. His window was open, his arms were on the window frame, and he was leaning forward. Pulling my throw blanket around my shoulders, I yanked up the sash.

"What did you just throw?" I asked him.

"Pencil topper," he said. "I tried with a paper clip first, but it didn't go far. It's down in our bushes now." He rested his chin in his hands. "How are you?"

I knew what he meant. "I've moved on from being freaked out about having everyone over to being freaked out about the fact that I might lose the election, but if I win, it will be because people think I'm a dog."

"Oh. You aren't freaked out about the project?"

"I can't really freak out about that properly until I finish my speech for student council elections."

Harry held up his phone, obviously rereading the text I'd just sent.

"That's not freaking out," I insisted. "That's just a help-ful reminder!"

"I didn't need the reminder," Harry said. "I'm working on the project."

"Harry, I can see that you've been gaming!"

"Lizzie—" Harry took a deep breath. "Look, I said I'm on it, okay?"

"I guess I'd rather send reminders than deal with this speech."

"What's so hard about it?" Harry asked. "Just say, 'I'm Lizzie, I'm organized and creative, I'm running for secre-tary, only a fool would vote for someone else.'"

"'And I'm not a dog.'"

"Yeah, I don't really know where that's coming from," Harry admitted.

"I swear that Rex and Ant's friends think Bella's name is Lizzie. They think 'Fetch Those Funds' is about an actual dog."

At the sound of her voice, Bella came over to the win-dow. I stroked her head and she settled down.

"So, like, they think the campaign is a joke?"

"I have no idea! *And* I told my mom I'd go to the meeting she has with the principal about this whole emotional support animal thing, and I don't even know if I really want Bella to come to school with me!"

"You don't?"

"No! But Mom told everyone that we're doing this, and everyone is, like, woo! And since Bella's my whole campaign strategy, I kind of have to go along with it . . ."

"Wait." Harry held up his hand.

I waited. I sometimes have to do that with Harry. It can take him a few moments to get his thoughts together. Finally, he put his hand down. "You *don't* want Bella to come to school?"

"Well . . ." Something about the way he emphasized the word *don't* sent a cold lump into my stomach, like I'd swallowed a frog.

"Don't you need her?" he asked.

"She's supposed to calm me down, but I actually think having her there would stress me out." The night air was cold; I pulled the blanket closer, burrito style.

I watched Harry thinking. The edges of his nostrils flared with his breath. Whatever was in his mind, it wasn't good. "You know this affects other people, too. Right?"

"What do you mean?"

"Lizzie, I'm *allergic* to your dog." Harry spoke slowly, his voice intense. "When my mom saw the hives on my arm, she seriously panicked. Don't you know what will happen if Bella gets permission to come to school with you?"

I thought for a moment. "That you'll have to sit on the other side of the room?"

"No. I'll have to *completely transfer* out of all the classes that I have with you." There was a pause. I guess Harry realized that I still wasn't quite getting the problem because he went on, "It means that I'll have to change my entire schedule and I'll be in new sections—possibly with different teachers—and that *sucks*."

"Maybe they'll change *my* schedule—"

"Well, then it sucks for *you*." Harry wasn't shouting. Harry doesn't shout. But it kind of felt like Harry was shouting. "And for me, because then we won't have classes together. The point is, I was willing to put up with whatever because I thought that you really needed Bella. Now you're telling me that you don't need to have a dog in the school, *and* that you don't really even *want* to bring her? And you're not telling anyone?"

"It's not that easy—"

"Yes it is! It *is* that easy. You just have to admit that you can't make everyone happy all the time. Just be honest; *it's not that hard.*"

Hot shame burned through me as he reached up and shut his window.

Everything turned blurry and tears spilled from my bottom lashes. The cold air chilled the tracks as they crept down my cheeks.

Slowly, I reached up and closed my window, too. Bella rested her head against my knee and let out a sigh. "What am I doing?" I whispered.

Harry said it was easy, but I really didn't know how to say, "Oh, sorry, you know this whole support animal thing isn't really important." It would look like I'd just used Bella for the election. And my mom—she'd get a huge *I told you so* from Mimi.

But Harry was a good friend, always. And he wasn't wrong about this.

My stupid tears were still stupidly falling on my stupid face, but I wasn't just sad. I was also teary because Harry was willing to put up with changing his whole schedule just because he thought Bella would help me.

He was good, and I was the worst.

I texted Monique: **Tell me I'm a good person.**

No reply.

I texted the same to Linden. **You are a good person** came the quick reply. **But I'm at a dorm meeting—talk later?** I clicked a thumbs-up and shoved the phone in my pocket.

Somehow I only felt worse.

Downstairs, Dad was parked on the couch, staring at his laptop, as usual.

"Where's Mom?"

Dad looked up at me. "Mom?" he repeated, as if he'd never heard of her.

Then I remembered—it was the second Tuesday of the month. "Book group," I said.

"Oh, right." Dad returned to his computer.

I wanted to go back upstairs, but somehow, I couldn't quite make myself move. The sadness had landed on me like a large, wet comforter, weighing me down.

After a moment, Dad looked up again. He cocked his head. "You okay?"

I couldn't quite make my mouth move, either, but I managed to lift one shoulder in a shrug.

"Do you want to . . ." Dad kind of paused, like maybe he thought I would help him out and start talking. But I couldn't. "Do you want to go get some ice cream?" he asked at last.

I wasn't in the mood, but I wasn't in the mood to stay at home, either. "Okay," I said.

In the car, Dad put on some of his terrible music. He refers to it as classic rock, which I guess makes it sound vaguely educational. It's the kind of music that people play air guitar to.

The weird thing about his music is, even though I never listen to it on purpose, I always know the words to about half of the songs. As the lights from streetlamps and businesses zipped by us, I realized I was softly singing along. After a moment, Dad joined in, and soon we were scream-singing, "I love rock and roll!" all the way to the ice-cream parlor.

In the summer, the line at Yo-Ho Pirate Cones stretches halfway down the block. Even on a chilly spring night like this, there were still plenty of people inside. Dad pushed open the door and held it for me, and that was when I saw Monique. She was facing away from me, but I'd know that hair and that sweatshirt with the cat on the back anywhere. She was seated at a small round table, and I knew what had to be in the bowl in front of her: raspberry sorbet.

Seated in the chair across was Rex, smiling as he spooned up a glob of hot fudge.

Dad looked confused as I stood in the open doorway. "Are we—"

I turned and walked out.

A moment later, I heard the bell over the door jingle as Dad let it fall and hurried after me. "I'm sorry," I whispered, but he just put his arm around me. It felt strong and warm as we made our way back to the car. Dad walked me to the passenger side and kissed me on the head before opening the door.

"Why don't we just drive for a while?" he suggested.

So we did.

Cold, cloudy days always make it hard to feel fully awake. I shuffled down the hallway under the fluorescent lights, barely registering the flow and swirl of students around me. But when I spotted Monique waiting by my locker, I froze. She noticed me and waved, but I turned and went into the bathroom, seeing nothing but Rex's happy face, smiling at Monique, in my mind.

Ignoring the vapers sitting on the floor (ew) and the

Makeup Queens at the sink, I stepped into a stall and locked the door behind me. I'd thought about it all night and I still couldn't believe that Monique hadn't told me that she was hanging out with Rex. I mean, were they on a *date*, or something? Whatever it was, she hadn't mentioned it, which really tells you something. She hadn't even answered my text about being a good person.

It just felt so *insulting*, like she didn't think I could handle it.

Can I handle it? I wondered. It was hard to separate the fact that Rex was my crush and the fact that Monique didn't tell me.

Which hurts more?

Does it matter?

A powerful wave of nausea hit me. I'd felt sick last night and still did when I woke up, but I didn't want to say anything to my mom. She'd probably insist I stay home, maybe even stay home *with* me, and it just felt easier to go to school. But now that I was here, I wasn't so sure.

The bell rang, so I flushed the toilet and went to the

sink to splash cold water on my face. I dried it with a scratchy brown paper towel that smelled like sour bark, then started to worry that my face smelled funky. I avoided my own gaze in the mirror and headed down the hallway to Dobbler's class. When I walked in, my queasy stomach sank to the floor. There was Monique, standing beside my desk, looking worried.

"Hey—are you okay?"

"I'm fine," I lied as I dropped my backpack on the floor and slid into my chair. Seats around me started filling up. Kids were clumped in twos and threes, joking around, chatting. Jacob was filming Dan trying (and failing) to do a viral dance. Cecily was braiding Mandy's hair while she frowned into her phone camera, watching instructions. Harry didn't even look in my direction as he sat in a new spot in the front right corner of the room.

"Okay, because you don't look fine," Monique said. "You look . . ."

"Hey!" Ant said cheerfully. "You ready for our—holy guacamole, what *happened* to you, you look *awful*."

"I'm *fine*," I snapped, and Monique gave me this raised-eyebrow look, then turned and stalked to her seat. My stomach—already on the floor—cut a hole in the linoleum and started digging toward the center of the earth.

"Uh . . . oooookaaaaaay." Ant looked confused. "Just so you know, I'm all set for the presentation."

"That's great, Ant."

I knew I was doing the worst possible thing: being angry and not saying anything. I knew that I should just ask Monique what was up with Rex and then pretend to be happy for her if necessary, but I just couldn't. I could *not*. Not right then. Besides, the second bell had already rung.

"Okay, class, everyone in your seats." Clapping twice, Ms. Dobbler strode toward her desk.

The class groaned and my stomach shot up from its visit to the earth's core. I had to swallow hard to keep it inside my body; my guts were churning like a washing machine, and I felt lightheaded.

My phone pinged.

Monique: **You okay?**

I could feel her staring at me, and I just couldn't take it. I was caught in a vise, and someone was leaning on the lever, trying to crush me into pulp.

My brain was in total power-save mode, but my body somehow stood up, and I half walked, half stumbled to my teacher's desk. "Ms. Dobbler?" I whispered.

"Back in your seat, Morris-Artino," she said.

"I'm just . . ." I put my hand on her desk to steady myself and swallowed hard. "May I go to the bathroom?"

"After the presentation." Snapping her fingers, she pointed to my seat.

"I really need to go now."

"After the presentation. But your group can present first."

First? Ugh. Ant smiled at me, but Harry barely glanced in my direction as he hauled himself out of his seat. I hurried to my desk and pulled my computer out of my backpack. Dobbler helped me hook it up to the smartboard, and I handed Harry a printout.

In a low voice, I told him, "I did the slides for you, and

I wrote a few paragraphs. You can just read them."

Harry didn't even look at the paper. "I'm not doing that."

"Are you ready?" Ms. Dobbler asked.

I shoved the paper at Harry, who swatted it away. I tried to force it into his hand, so he grabbed it, wadded it up, and tossed it in the trash. "Oops," he said.

"If we flunk this, it's on your head," I hissed.

"It's *on my head*? Like a curse?"

"Or a hat," Ant added, completely unhelpfully. "Or a tiara?"

"We're all waiting," Dobbler singsonged.

"Don't tell me Lizzie's group isn't ready!" Jacob said, and Dan gave him a high five.

"We're ready," Ant said.

"No, we aren't," I whispered.

"Lizzie," Ant replied, "we're as ready as we are going to be. Let's go." And with that, he stepped to the front of the class. He started by explaining the importance of the *Epic of Gilgamesh*, how it influenced other epics that came after it. Then he gave a dramatic reading of one of the scenes. He had slides. It was solid.

Then I gave my part, about how people discovered the epic and learned to translate cuneiform. "And now, Harry has some slides." I clicked onto the slide presentation that I'd prepared. My face felt sweaty, and it somehow activated that disgusting paper towel smell.

"No, I don't," Harry said.

"Yes, you do!" I chirped.

"Lizzie," Ant whispered. "Just let Harry do his thing."

"Harry doesn't have a thing!" I whispered as the room started to spin. I grabbed the edge of Dobbler's desk. "I don't feel so—" And then the scrambled eggs and orange juice that had been threatening to make their way up my throat finally did, pouring aggressively into Ms. Dobbler's trash can.

She dropped her clipboard as the class exploded into mayhem. "Disgusting!" Dan shouted, and Mandy got up and hurried to the back of the room, as if my barf might get up and try to splatter her.

Dobbler was yelling for everyone to stay in their seats, but people were shouting and shooting video. In the chaos, I felt a strong hand on my arm and I heard a voice say, "I'm taking her to the nurse."

"Go!" Dobbler shooed me out of the room as she shouted, "I want everyone in their seats now!"

The pandemonium died away as the door closed behind us and Monique steered me toward the nurse's office, murmuring, "You're okay. It's okay. You just need to lie down." My face was wet with sick and tears and paper towel smell, and all I could think about was the fact that I could never show my face in this school again.

I like the nurse's office. It's quiet. It's clean. No one was in the second cot, so I got to do nothing but stare up at the ceiling, which has the kind of patterned tiles that you can imagine faces and scenes in. Like watching clouds.

Because I'd thrown up, the nurse called my mom and all

I had to do was wait until she showed up. In the pattern of the ceiling tile above, a river flowed, then disappeared. A frog revealed itself, then became a lizard with a long tail. For once, my mind did not spin out stories of endless disasters. Maybe because it knew my life was actually over.

"Knock, knock." A figure in black appeared in the doorway to the little room. "I just thought I'd check on you." Ms. Dobbler pulled the one metal chair closer to my cot and looked down at me. There was something about her eyes. They were soft, as if she wanted to hear what I had to say. "How do you feel?"

"Not good." I wanted to ask about the project, but I didn't dare.

"A little embarrassed, maybe?" she suggested.

"Not at all," I told her. "On an unrelated note, I'm going to be moving to Antarctica soon. Like, probably tomorrow. We should probably say goodbye now. I'll be living there under a new identity, so don't expect to stay in touch."

She nodded. "I see. Getting a fresh start?"

"I can't come back to this school. Ever."

"Well . . ." She adjusted her slacks. "I'll miss you."

I pulled the pillow from behind my head and pressed it over my face. It's actually kind of comforting to mash your face in a pillow. Gently, Ms. Dobbler peeled it away and peeked in at me, still wearing that sympathetic smile. "I wanted to apologize," she said. "I should have let you go to the bathroom. I should've realized that you, of all people, were not trying to get out of doing your presentation. I should have known you really weren't feeling well."

"I should apologize to *you*," I told her. "I know I made your trash can smell like barf eggs. I'll bet everyone could smell it."

"I didn't smell it."

"Really?"

"Well . . . not until I cleaned it up."

I mashed the pillow back onto my face. On the bright side, I didn't have to give my student council speech tomorrow—there was no possible way I was getting up in front of everyone after this!

"At least your presentation was memorable."

When I pulled the pillow from my face, I saw Ms. Dobbler's little smile had gotten knotted up in the corner of her mouth, like she was trying not to laugh. "So. What's going on? Are you sick, or is there something else?"

It was weird to be talking to the world's scariest teacher as if she were just a normal person, but I found myself very comfortably chatting with Ms. Dobbler. "Did you know that I'm running for class secretary? I'm going to lose the election so badly. I think it's possible I will get a *negative* number of votes."

"People don't vote for people based on whether or not they vomit."

"I'm sorry—you *do* know that we're in middle school right now, right? People will literally vote or not vote for you based on whether you're wearing the wrong *socks*." This was not an exaggeration. Last year, Oliver Romero lost class treasurer because he came to school in Thomas the Tank Engine socks. It was so petty.

"Okay," Ms. Dobbler said after a moment, "let's say that this does affect your campaign—so what?"

I really, really hate it when grown-ups use that voice that implies that your problems are just super small compared to theirs. "Seriously? I'll lose! It'll be humiliating!"

"It's never fun to lose," Ms. Dobbler agreed. "I get it. That will be hard and you will be sad, but do you know what?"

"Are you going to tell me that I can handle it?"

"You might not want to, but you would if you needed to."

"I will be handling it from Antarctica."

"Losing class secretary wouldn't be a catastrophe."

"Of course not, because I'll be in Antarctica."

"You don't even know for sure that you'll lose. You can't predict the future. You can't read peoples' minds. The first President Bush once vomited on the prime minister of Japan, Lizzie, and he still got a presidential library. Look on the bright side—at least you didn't vomit on Prime Minister Miyazawa."

I tried to imagine this. "Did that really happen?"

She held up a hand. "I swear."

I sighed. "I know grown-ups always say things will get better and middle school stuff doesn't matter in the long run. But . . . it just feels like things keep happening and getting worse, and I'm just, like, floating down this terrible river, getting bumped against rocks and rolled around in swirls and—like maybe I'll end up drowned or going over the edge of a waterfall or *both*. You know?"

She nodded. "That is the way it feels sometimes. But you won't drown, Lizzie."

"How do you know?"

"Because, from what I've seen, you're a good swimmer." Rising to her feet, she dragged the metal chair back into place, then looked at me. "By the way, your group got an A on the project."

"What?" I lifted myself onto my elbows. *"How?"*

"That video game Harry made based on the *Epic of Gilgamesh* was really something. Have you played all twenty-seven levels?"

"Uh . . . no?"

"Well, your group was a great example of everyone con-tributing their strengths to the assignment." Ms. Dobbler ran her fingers through her perfect hair. "Great work. Great *teamwork*."

Great teamwork?

Huh.

I was nearly finished with the ginger ale that Mom brought me when she pulled the car into our driveway. She turned off the ignition and we sat in the quiet for a moment.

"How do you feel?"

I took another sip of the sweet, spicy soda. It burned a little in my throat as I screwed the top back onto the green bottle. "I feel okay."

"Do you want me to call the doctor?"

"No."

"Was it anxiety?"

I didn't want to lie, so I just said, "I felt sick. I feel better now."

Mom nodded, touched my hand, and looked at me with a lovey face. She does stuff like that a lot—it's kind of weird and corny. But I guess it's nice, too. I let her stare at me for another moment, until finally she opened the car door and we headed toward the house.

Bella must have heard us coming because I could hear her toenails clicking excitedly against the floor inside. When we opened the door, she was wagging and wiggling uncontrollably. I gave her a hug and she put her head on my shoulder. Definitely the best part of the day.

Mom dropped her keys on the table and hung her purse on the hook. "Why don't you go upstairs and rest?"

"That's the plan." Bella followed, passing me halfway up the stairs.

"I'll check on you later," Mom called.

I paused at the top of the stairs. Instead of heading left, toward my room, I turned right.

Linden's room was in its usual state of chaos. Worse

than usual, actually. Bella trotted right in and started sniffing around. A pile of papers balanced precariously on a fuzzy beanbag chair. There was a cup collection on her bedside table, along with a puddle of coins. Stuffed animals were strewn everywhere, along with discarded clothes. Her bed was unmade. It looked like she might come home any minute, like she'd never left.

I wanted to text her and tell her what had happened at school, but it just wasn't the same. I hadn't realized how much boarding school would change things—how different it would be, having a sister who didn't live at home most of the time.

Bella sat on a workbook in the middle of Linden's blue rug and looked at me with that cocked-head curious expression she wears.

"Come on," I told her, and headed to my room. I changed into my pajamas and tucked myself into bed, enjoying the afternoon sunbeam that fell across my pillow. Even though I wasn't really sick with the flu or a cold or anything, throwing up always makes me feel tired, so I closed my eyes.

I didn't wake up until my mom knocked at my door.

"Hey," she said, "you have a visitor," and a moment later Monique burst into my room and flopped on the edge of my bed.

"Don't freak out," she said.

"Okay, saying that is a good way to get me to start freaking out. What happened?"

Monique tapped her phone, then held it out to me. It was a boomerang of me barfing over and over. "Harry showed it to me; it's all over Picbomb," she said. "Oh, hi, Bella."

I pulled my blankets over my head.

"What is it?" I heard my mom ask, and I guess Monique showed her because she said, "Are you *serious*? Someone posted this to social media?"

"You should sue them," Monique suggested.

"Who was it?" Mom demanded.

"This guy Jacob Underhill, from our social studies class."

"I'm calling the school," Mom announced. "I want a meeting with his mother!"

I yanked the blanket off my face. "Mom, no!"

"You *should* do that!" Monique insisted.

"You be quiet," I told her. "Don't encourage her. Mom, please. I don't want to get into this—it's only going to make everything worse!"

Mom scowled. "Well. I'm bringing it up when we meet with Principal Yeoh, which by the way is the day after tomorrow."

"Ugh, I totally forgot."

"Lizzie gives her campaign speech Friday morning," Monique said.

"What time?" Mom asked.

"Beginning of flex—second period."

"Our meeting is first thing; she'll be done."

"I can't handle this right now!" I groaned.

Mom and Monique looked at each other. "Okay," Mom said. "I'll let you rest some more."

"I'll just be here for another minute," Monique told her. Once my mom had shut the door, my best friend turned to me and said, "Listen—April reposted that stupid GIF;

that's part of why it's going around. She added this." Monique held up her screen to show the GIF with a banner over it that read RETCH THOSE FUNDS!

"She is the *worst*!"

"I told you! But here's what I'm thinking." Tapping her screen, Monique held up a poster with the headline, APRIL PEED IN BED UNTIL FIFTH GRADE. "I also made one that says she used to practice kissing on her teddy bear, Mr. Bumbles."

"Is that true?"

"Does it matter?"

"We can't post that!"

"Well maybe *you* can't, but I can," Monique said.

"Please don't."

"Lizzie, you don't know how to crush people, but I do, and April needs to be crushed!"

"You just want to beat April! Do you even care about what *I* want? I'm not even sure I want to be in this election anymore, Monique!"

Her mouth clamped shut, and we just sat there staring at each other. My feet were tucked under Bella, who was curled, catlike, at the foot of my bed. After a long, silent moment, Monique stood up and walked out.

"Monique," I called, but not loud enough for her to hear.

Reaching out, I touched Bella's velvety ear. "I can't do it," I told her. "Bella—I can't get up there and make a speech and have everyone watching that video of me barfing all over the place." I shook my head and whispered, "I just can't."

Bella must have sensed something in my tone of voice because she sat up. Then, gently, she put her paw on my arm. Exactly like a friend would do, telling me that it was okay.

"You'll like me no matter what happens, right?" I asked. She licked my arm.

I scooted back down into my covers, and Bella burrowed beside me. The blankets rose and fell with our breathing as I listened to the silence in my room. I thought about what Ms. Dobbler had said, about how I'm a good swimmer. *Maybe this is part of swimming*, I thought. *Knowing when enough is enough.*

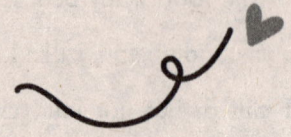

CHAPTER NINE

Ephebiphobia—fear of adolescents

To be fair, I find adolescents terrifying, and I am one. Just picturing the auditorium filled with middle schoolers while I make my speech... ugh.

Even an auditorium full of clowns wouldn't be as scary.

"Where are you headed?" Mom asked as I slipped into my jacket. It was Thursday evening; I had stayed home from school. I had felt too sick to face everyone when I woke up, but after a day in bed reading, I was feeling a lot better.

"I was going to take Bella for a walk."

"You sure? I can do it."

"I got it. Back in a while."

"Take your phone."

"Mom, when do I ever forget my phone?" I clipped the leash onto Bella's harness and we left out the side door.

The morning's gloom had cleared, and the wind rippled new leaves wherever it could find them. The cold air tried to slip inside the neck of my jacket; I pulled my scarf closer around my neck. Overhead, white clouds raced across a deep blue sky. Bella's tags jingled as she trotted happily beside me. Mr. Everson was out in his yard, mulching the flower beds at the edge of his perfect still-green lawn. He waved and smiled, and I waved back.

Three doors down, our neighbors' twin daughters, Katie and Sophie Neary, were playing one of their strange five-year-old games—Katie was dressed as a bat and

Sophie was dressed as a witch, and they seemed to be making a fortress of sticks.

None of these people know that I barfed in school, I thought. *Unless they have Picbomb, which I doubt.*

We paused for Bella to sniff things a few times, then finally made our way to the edge of the cemetery. Bella stopped suddenly, staring intently at a squirrel near the gate. I was about to tell her that we weren't going in when I caught sight of someone waving. It was Ant. He was on top of the tomb again. I nearly turned and ran out of there, but the minute Bella spotted him, I had no choice—we were going in.

Ant jumped down and petted Bella. He looked up at me, squinting one eye in the sun. "How's it going?" he asked. "Missed you today. You okay?"

"I'm better." I felt the heat creep into my cheeks. "I'm pretty embarrassed, though."

"Eh," he said with a shrug, "everybody barfs."

I gave him a doubtful look.

"Not usually as *dramatically*," he admitted. "And they

don't usually get frog-marched out of the class by their best friend, but as my dad always says, 'If you're going to go, go big.'"

He stood up and the three of us started walking down the main path.

"I don't really think that applies in this case."

"It absolutely does!"

I laughed a little. Keeping his hands shoved deep into his jacket pockets, Ant cocked his elbow and poked me in the arm. There was a large weeping cherry tree at the center of the cemetery. Its bark was smooth and gray, like elephant hide, and its branches bent soft pink blooms that swayed, dripping pink petals in the breeze. We walked beneath it, and Ant looked up, so I did, too. You could see pieces of the blue sky beyond the flowers.

"You know, Lizzie," he said slowly, still looking at the sky. "Everyone does dumb stuff sometimes." And then he looked at me and traced his finger over the scar that cut through his eyebrow.

My face flushed with embarrassment. "Yeah, but, I

mean, that's not . . ." I could not think of a single thing to say.

"You know about this, right? I mean, everyone knows. Everyone thinks they know."

I started to nod, then shook my head.

"It's okay." His voice was gentle. "I know what you've heard. Everyone thinks that I set off a bunch of fireworks and nearly killed me and Nico. And that's not . . ." He shrugged again. "I mean, it doesn't matter what they think. But the point is that I'm still here. I still have friends, you know?"

"That's different."

"No, it isn't."

"It is," I insisted.

"If anything, mine is much worse. Everyone thinks I did a seriously stupid thing and nearly blew my face off. You just got sick."

"But you're . . ." I wasn't quite sure what to say. "You were doing something dangerous. So that makes it seem kind of cool to people."

"Did *you* think it was cool?"

"No."

"Okay, then."

"But I'm not cool, so nobody cares what I think is cool."

"*I* do." Ant looked down at his feet, and I was speech-less again. Finally, he cleared his throat and went on, "Lots of people avoided me after that. Nico's parents wouldn't let us hang out again. Ever. They sent him to another school. And he was my best friend. Nobody even knows . . ."

Silence hung between us. "Knows what?" I asked.

Ant looked up. He looked into my eyes, and I forced myself not to turn away. "You won't tell anyone."

"I won't."

"I know; that's what I just said. It probably doesn't even matter, anyway. It used to seem like it did. But I know everyone says it was all my fault, which maybe it was. The part that was definitely my fault is that it was my idea. I knew my grandfather had some fireworks in the base-ment. We were going to set them off on the Fourth of July.

But it was still June, and I swear, it felt like waiting for Christmas Eve. It never seemed to get any closer."

"I know what that's like."

"So I figured . . . my grandpa wouldn't miss one little package of roman candles, right? Even if he did notice, he might think it got left out of the bag at the store, or something. When I mentioned the idea to Nico, it was all over. He wanted those roman candles. He told me that if I didn't get them, he'd come in and steal them himself. He told me that he couldn't be friends with someone who was afraid of getting in trouble. That I was dumb for being afraid of an old man. All he wanted was to have a video of us setting those things off that he could show everyone."

"Oh no."

"Yeah. So we went out to the big field near Finnian Lake and I made him pick up all the dead leaves and twigs and stuff so at least we wouldn't set the place on fire. Then I said how my grandfather and I did this every year, and that you have to be very careful and put the roman candle in the ground at an angle and keep clear once you light it. The package had three roman candles, and we did the first one exactly as I said, and it was super cool. We got a good video of it, and everything. Then Nico decided to hold one while it went off. I told him to point it away from himself. So he said, 'Okay, film me.' So I said okay. And then I don't really remember it that well, but Nico was holding the roman candle and I was holding up the tablet we were recording with. He lit it, and then he told me something about the tablet, like he wanted a different angle. And he gestured for me to move, but I guess he forgot he had the roman candle in his hand because it blasted off right at my face."

I put my hands over my face and cringed. "He pointed it *at* you?"

"Not on purpose. At first, I couldn't see or hear. I thought I'd been blinded. I just fell to the ground holding my eye, thinking about what an idiot I was while Nico ran, he *ran* screaming to get his mom. She called 911 and then drove back. Luckily, she's a nurse and she kept pressure on my face and made me keep still until the EMTs got there in the ambulance. And the whole time, Nico was crying, totally freaking out. He told me later that my face was covered in blood and he thought I was dying. But, you know, it turned out that the blast had missed my eye and had just clipped my eyebrow and forehead. Ten stitches and I was out of the hospital.

"I was in *so much* trouble, though. And my grandfather"—Ant sighed—"he blamed himself. That was the worst part. He got rid of all the fireworks and then, I think, he got really depressed. He said he didn't blame me, that I was just a kid. He blamed himself for letting me know where they were. And that felt worse than anything."

A pink petal fell from the tree, twirling to the ground, landing between us. "What happened with Nico?" I asked.

"He begged me not to tell anyone that he'd messed up. So I said that I put the candle in the ground but not deep enough and it fell over and shot at me. Nobody really cared about what exactly happened. Dumb kids with fireworks— enough said. And I was the one with the scar. So now I'm

That Idiot Who Played with Fireworks. Everyone thinks I have bad judgment, and I don't blame them. Especially my parents. That's why they won't let me get a dog. They don't trust me. They don't believe I can change."

I took this in. Neither of us spoke for a long time. "Why do you come here?" I asked.

He gestured back toward the small tombstone near the crypt. "My grandfather. He died last year, so I come here sometimes."

I didn't know what to say. "I'm sorry."

"Yeah. I mean, he was pretty old. But I still really miss him."

"And I'm sorry about the . . . other stuff."

"Yeah." Ant nodded. "But, Lizzie, that's the thing—it's kind of a filter. Like, the people who judge me without getting to know me? It's okay. I don't need them to be my friends. And Nico? I guess I found out what he was all about, right?"

"I judged you," I admitted.

"Okay. But you still got to know me. And now I got an

A on my project and I have a B+ in social studies, thanks to you. My parents might just get me that dog."

"Monique says you're kind of a chaos agent," I admitted. "But not in a bad way."

"She's hilarious."

"Ant . . . Thanks for telling me all of that. That story. And about your grandfather."

"Hold still," he said, and reached toward my hair. Gently, he pulled a petal from just in front of my left ear. Holding it up, a slow smile spread across his face. "Earring," he said.

"How long has it been there?" I asked.

"The whole time."

"You let me stand there with a flower petal in my hair, like an idiot?"

"I thought it was pretty," he said, and I swear, it felt like the time I was at the ocean and a giant wave came and knocked me over—for a moment, I wasn't sure which way was up, until I finally hit the ground and kicked toward the surface. Same exact feeling, only not scary.

It didn't feel scary at all.

⤲

I should have told her. I realized it the minute I walked into the school office and sat down next to my mom in one of the uncomfortable brown vinyl chairs. *I had all day yesterday and all morning . . . the whole drive over to tell her.* Feeling my gaze, she looked over at me and smiled, and my stomach lurched. *Why do I even* eat *breakfast?*

It was half an hour to first bell, and we had arrived for our meeting with Principal Yeoh.

Just get through this, I told myself. I felt my folded-up speech in my pocket. *Worry about one thing at a time.*

"Good morning, Lizzie Morris-Artino." Ms. Linwood, the school secretary, smiled at me from behind the counter. She used to work in the elementary school, so she knows a good chunk of the seventh and eighth graders. She still wears silly patterned shirts in bright colors and tells us to "make good choices" in the morning announcements, but I think most people secretly love it.

I leaned my head against Mom's shoulder. "This will be good," she said.

I nodded and thought hopefully, *Maybe they'll tell us no, and I won't have to say anything at all.*

The bell rang and after a moment, Ms. Linwood started reading the morning announcements. A girls' soccer game. A half day next Wednesday. Class officer speeches during second period. "And don't forget to log in to your account on StudentSpace to vote for class officers before lunchtime."

Mom looked over at me. "That's you, right?" she whispered.

I shook my head. "No."

Mom's eyebrows drew together. "Aren't you giving a speech?" she asked, but before I could answer, Principal Yeoh's office door opened, and he smiled at us.

"Ms. Morris-Artino?" he asked, holding out a hand. He and my mother shook hands and said the usual grown-up stuff about what a pleasure it was to see him again, and then he smiled at me, and said, "Hi, Lizzie."

"Hi, Mr. Yeoh."

"Excited about today?" he asked, and I said, "Oh, yeah," hoping I didn't sound too sarcastic.

Just as we were about to step into his office, a movement caught my eye, and I saw Ant standing at the window that looked out onto the front hallway. Waving at me, he held up his phone and gave me a thumbs-up, whatever that meant. I shooed at him to get to class, and he nodded and scurried away.

Mr. Yeoh had already slipped into the chair behind his desk and gestured to us to have a seat in the two chairs across from his desk. They were about five million times nicer than the ones in the main office. I guess it's usually parents who sit in here so they get the good chairs.

"So!" Mr. Yeoh began brightly. "I've already spoken to Vice Principal Walker, and I understand that Lizzie would like to bring an emotional support animal to school." He reached for a pencil and began twirling it as he leaned back. "Why don't you tell me about that."

"Lizzie has been dealing with severe anxiety this year." Mom pulled a manila folder from her black leather tote and flipped it open. "As you know, her sister left for boarding school this past fall, and Lizzie's had a tough adjustment. Bella, our dog, is a calming influence on Lizzie. I've had her certified as an Emotional Support Animal." She handed several sheets of paper to Mr. Yeoh, who took them, frowning slightly.

"I don't know this organization," he said.

"They're national," Mom replied.

"National as in, you got this online?" Mr. Yeoh didn't say this meanly. He said it like he thought it was kind of sweet, as if he'd seen a lot of parents do whatever they thought it would take to help their kids.

But Mom didn't smile. "I also renewed my driver's license online. There's nothing wrong with doing business online."

Mr. Yeoh placed the papers on his desk and said, "Let's leave this for a minute. Lizzie, I'd like to hear from you."

This took me completely by surprise. I guess I'm just

so used to grown-ups saying no to things that it hadn't occurred to me that he might actually want to hear me out.

"Go on," Mom said, smiling. "Tell him how you feel calmer and less anxious when Bella is around."

"Um . . . I think you just told him," I said, and her smile wavered.

Mr. Yeoh pursed his lips. "Do you have any concerns?" he asked.

"Well . . . maybe, yeah. I'm concerned about my friend, Harry. He's allergic to Bella, and he's worried that he'll have to change out of the classes that we have together."

"Hm." The yellow pencil twirled, then twirled again.

"Well," Mom said after a moment. "That might be inconvenient for Harry, but I think it would be worth it if it helps you feel better. I'm sure he'll understand."

I pictured Harry's face on the night I admitted that I wasn't even sure I wanted Bella to come to school, and I felt my cheeks burn, like a spotlight had been turned on me.

I'm a bad friend, I thought. I looked at my mom, who was wearing an expectant smile. I hated to let her down, but I was going to have to let someone down.

I can't make everyone happy all the time, I told myself, and then, out loud, I heard myself say, "I'm sorry."

Mr. Yeoh sat up straighter in his chair, but Mom was perfectly still. They were both silent until the principal said, "What are you sorry about?"

I turned to my mom. "I'm sorry, but I don't think it's a good idea to bring Bella to school."

"Doesn't she make you feel better?" she asked.

"Yes. Yes, absolutely—at home, she makes me feel better. But she's not ready to come to school with me, Mom. She's not trained yet, and I actually find having her around to be pretty stressful."

"But . . . don't you need support?"

"I *have* support. I have Monique. And I have Harry. And even if I didn't . . . I . . . I'm a good swimmer."

"What?"

"I just . . . I think lots of people really need therapy

dogs. But I'm not sure that's me. At least not now, and not this dog."

My mother stared as if she was having trouble recognizing me.

Mr. Yeoh looked from me to my mom, then back to me. "Perhaps we should revisit this at a later date," he said.

It took Mom another moment to process what had just happened. "I'm sorry to have wasted your time," she said to Mr. Yeoh, and she slid the manila folder back into her tote bag. Standing up, she reached out to shake his hand.

"It wasn't a waste at all," he said. To me, he added, "I think this was very important."

Nodding, I whispered, "Thank you."

Then I followed my mom into the main office. "Okay," she said, turning to me. "I guess that's it. I'll see you tonight."

"Mom, I'm sorry. I know you're just trying to help, but what you're doing with Bella and everything, it's just making things worse, and I—"

Shaking her head, Mom held up her palm. "Just—just

let me think about this, okay? I'll see you tonight." I stood there watching as she walked out of the office and through the front doors.

"Should I get you a pass to your first period class?" asked Ms. Linwood. I turned around slowly. "Do you need a pass?" she repeated.

"Yeah. Yes."

She wrote one out, then tore it off the pad and handed it to me. "There you go, Lizzie. And good luck today!"

I took a deep breath. *I'm a good swimmer*, I told myself. *I'm going to lose. It's going to be embarrassing. But I can handle this.* Ms. Linwood's smile was so sweet and hopeful that I just took the pass and said, "Thanks."

"And so that's why I think you should vote for me," Milo Salsbury said into the microphone. "I can't wait to be eighth grade vice president." The crowd in the auditorium broke into wild applause, and I shifted in my seat. Milo was incredibly popular, but he was also running unopposed. So far, we'd heard speeches from Charlie Jones, Lily Yao, and Tate Rodgers, who were all running for eighth grade class president. They were all decent choices, and I wasn't sure who would win.

And I wasn't running at all.

Again, I touched the speech in my pocket. It was only two lines: "My name is Lizzie Morris-Artino. I want to thank everyone who has supported me, but I have decided to withdraw my name from consideration as next year's eighth grade class secretary."

I was filled with dread, but I was excited, too. Telling my mom that I didn't want Bella to come to school with me had given me a boost.

Looking out into the audience, I caught sight of Monique sitting with Alison and Trina, two girls from our math class. I looked away. I didn't want to think about what Monique was going to say.

Vice Principal Walker stepped up to the podium. "We will now hear from our eighth grade class secretary candidates," she announced. "First, please welcome April McDonough."

April stood up and smiled for the audience, giving her hair a dramatic flip over one shoulder. Then she smoothed her fuzzy sweater over the front of her pink skirt and stepped to the podium.

I hadn't even thought about getting dressed up for the speeches. I was just wearing a green shirt and a gray pair of sweatpants. I adjusted the shirt so that it hid the stain near the waist.

"Hello, seventh grade—next year's eighth graders!" April said into the microphone. "I'm April McDonough. I'm running for class secretary, and I want to make one thing clear . . . I'm not a dog." She turned to flash a look at me as everyone erupted into laugher. "Some people have been trying to get your vote by using a cute animal in their campaign," she went on. "But the fact is, we're voting for class secretary. And needing an emotional support dog shouldn't be the reason why you vote for anyone. In fact . . . some people might even think it's a reason *not* to vote for someone. If you get anxious so easily, maybe leadership isn't for you."

A dark cloud lowered over my vision. My nerves melted; my whole body felt as if someone had poured lava down my throat. *It doesn't matter*, I told myself. *You're dropping out.* That was my brain speaking. Some part of me heard it, but it felt like it was coming from far away.

"But, unlike *some* people, I'm not here to talk about dogs! Secretary is a great position, and it deserves someone who will take it seriously. And that's me. April McDonough." April gave a little curtsey, like she was in front of the king or something, and then went back to her seat, smirking at me all the way.

I know that Vice Principal Walker must have announced me. I know I must have stepped up to the podium. But the next thing I remember is standing at the microphone, pulling my two-sentence speech from my pocket. My hands were trembling. I placed the speech on the podium. I read the first sentence. "My name is Lizzie Morris-Artino," I said. Then I paused. Someone coughed.

Someone else shifted in their chair. I had to force myself to go on. "I want to thank everyone who has supported me, but I . . ."

My brain gave me an image: that smug smile on April's face after I dropped out.

My whole body felt hot. My vision narrowed. "I want to say a few things. First, I'm not a dog, either." There were a few nervous laughs. "And I just want to make clear that some people need emotional support animals and service animals, and there's nothing wrong with that. Sometimes I feel anxious. I'll bet everyone here does. And anyone who thinks there's something wrong with people who get anxious, well . . . maybe they shouldn't be representing the eighth grade class, because our class officers are supposed to represent *everybody*, not judge any of us."

Someone clapped a little, and a few more people joined. Then it was quiet again.

"My dog isn't an emotional support animal, but that's mostly because my dog is still learning. But none of that has to do with this election! This election is about class secretary, and I'm running because I want to go on the eighth grade class trip. I know it can be amazing, and we can have a lot of fun with the fundraising. I'm thinking of candygrams, and a spaghetti supper, and maybe even a trivia contest. Other schools have raised lots of money with fundraisers like those, and I've already planned out how we can make them happen." I looked out into the audience. I could see Monique sitting forward in her chair. "I'm not perfect, but I know I'll be good at this." I turned to flash a smile at April, then leaned back to the microphone. "And gosh, April, would it have killed you to keep it positive?"

"Yeah, *April*!" someone shouted. It was Ant. Everyone around him laughed. I glanced at Monique, who held up her hand, palm out, then curled her fingers into a fist. *Crush*, she mouthed.

There was only one thing left to say. "Let's fetch those funds!" Monique punched the air as Ant stood up to applaud. Then Harry stood. Then a bunch of other people.

It was a standing ovation. I raised my voice over the cheers. "I'm Lizzie, and I hope to be your next class secretary!"

CHAPTER TEN

Alethophobia—fear or dislike of the truth

Oh, boy. I'm trying to get over this. They say that the truth will set you free. But it also might really freak you out.

When the weather's nice, we're allowed to eat lunch on the patio, which is a brick square at the center of the school building. It doesn't get much sun, but there's a big tree and you can look up at the sky, which is nice. It's pretty small, so kids with a ton of friends usually take the big tables in the lunchroom, which means that the patio is relatively quiet. Today, I couldn't deal with the lunchroom—the yelling, the boys tossing grapes at one another, the public humiliation of being the girl who barfed into a trash can, the girl who lost the election—so I headed out to the patio. The tables were full, so I sat on one of the low brick walls along the edge.

I unwrapped the lunch my mom had made me: a turkey sandwich with apple slices, sun-dried tomatoes, and chipotle mayo. If I had made the sandwich, it would have been turkey on bread with maybe mustard. But Mom has to turn everything into some kind of television cooking competition where they give you a bunch of random ingredients and you're supposed to make it into something delicious. And it *was* delicious.

"Mind if I sit here?" Harry gestured to the empty bricks beside me.

"Of course," I said.

"'Of course' you mind or 'of course' I can sit here?"

I rolled my eyes. "Please, Harry," I said.

Pulling a napkin from his lunch bag, he dusted off the

bricks and then sat gingerly down. He pulled an orange from the bag and frowned at it.

"I got it," I told him, and he passed it over.

"Thanks."

He watched as I sank a fingernail into the skin and then pulled it away from the juicy fruit.

"I don't know how you do that without mangling it," he said as I handed it back to him.

"One of my many skills," I told him.

He pulled off a section and held it out to me. I accepted it as he pulled off another and popped it into his mouth. "Harry," I said as he chewed, "thanks for your work on our social studies project."

He shrugged. "I told you that I had it covered."

"I know. And I—I'm really sorry I didn't listen. I'm sorry I didn't trust you."

"It's okay," he said. "I'm sorry I got so mad the other night. I've been thinking about it, and I know how hard it is—"

"I told my mom and Principal Yeoh that I don't want to bring Bella to school," I said.

He stared at me. "Lizzie, you—"

"No; it's okay. It's the truth; I don't want to. And you were right, I hadn't thought it all the way through. I needed to be honest with everyone."

"How did your mom take it?"

"Not well."

"She'll deal. She just wants to help."

"I know," I told him. "And I get that. It might take time, but—"

There was a loud bang from the double doors as Monique burst through them shouting, "Lizzie!"

Everyone turned to stare at her.

"Mind your own business," she snapped at them. Then she took a deep breath and walked—well, I guess *calmly* was what she was going for, but it looked more like she was trying to contain the helium of a thousand balloons—over to Harry and me. Leaning toward my ear, she hissed, "I've been looking for you all over the place! Don't make a scene."

"Uh, okay," I said as Harry blurted, "Too late."

Monique squeezed between the two of us. "I just got back from the dentist. I was in the office, and Ms. Linwood was there, and she gave me a pass and then she said, 'Aren't you friends with Lizzie Morris-Artino,' and I said that yes I was, and then she said, 'Hm,' and gave a little smile, and I was like, 'What? What is it?' and then she kind of tilted her computer monitor toward me—no, shut up, don't say something nerdy—"

This last comment was directed at Harry, who looked as if he might launch into some complaint about the schools' computers and/or internet security. He frowned but stayed quiet, and Monique went on.

"And she gestured for me to look at her screen and so I did and, *Lizzie*—" She looked around, and then dropped her voice to a whisper. "You *won*."

"What?" Harry asked, full volume. "She won what?"

Monique shushed him and looked around again as if Harry had just compromised national security, but nobody was even glancing in our direction. Then she looked at me, her dark eyes wide, her shoulders hunched forward, and an excited smile taking over her face. "Lizzie won the election!"

"That's . . . that's impossible!" I said.

Monique shook her head. "I saw it. I saw it, Lizzie! But Ms. Linwood made me promise not to tell—they're not announcing it until the end of the day."

"But . . . how?" I asked.

"I have no idea," Monique said.

We stared at each other for a moment. Then, slowly, our eyes shifted toward Harry, who was picking a dead brown leaf from the boxwood bush.

"What did you do?" I demanded.

Harry did a Who, me? gesture, and Monique narrowed her eyes at him. "Harry," she warned, "did you do some rogue hacker-boy thing and get into the school's computer system?"

"What? No!" He held up his hands. "No, no, no! I mean, I did do something, but nothing bad. I just took that video of you, Lizzie, the one where you're throwing up. The one with the caption, 'Retch Those Funds?' and

I kind of animated it so that it looked like you were barfing dollar bills. And then I . . . I sent it to Ant."

Monique and I looked at each other. "And . . . what did he do with it?" I asked.

"Some social media stuff, I assume," Harry said.

"How did you not know?" I asked Monique.

Monique yanked out her phone and started tapping at the screen. "I haven't checked it since Wednesday night. I mean, we'd kind of had a fight and—" Her mouth dropped open.

"What?" I snatched the phone from her.

The screen showed Ant's Picbomb story, which was a carousel—the first image was the GIF of me barfing dollar bills under the banner LIZZIE'S GONNA RAISE SO MUCH MONEY IT'S *SICK*!

"I like how he added music," Harry said as Lil Wayne's song "Money on My Mind" played in the background.

The next image was a screenshot of the schedule I'd made for our project, and so were the next three, showing our progress. The last was a short video of Ant, speaking right to the camera.

"Hey, everyone," he said. "I want to say something about this election we've got going for class officers. I know a lot of you don't care about it, but I wanted to give a shout-out for my friend Lizzie. I didn't really know her before this year, but we've been working on a project together and she's mad organized. And she cares. Like, she texts me twice a day about this stuff. So I just wanted to say, you know, that she'll be really great as class secretary; you should vote for her."

I looked at Monique. "It's been shared a hundred and seventy-two times," she said.

Harry was staring down at the phone with his eyebrows lifted. "That was pretty good," he said at last.

"So, like"—I glanced from Harry to Monique, who was smiling and shaking her head—"I won?" I asked.

"You did," Monique said.

And that was when I remembered that Monique didn't even know I'd tried to drop out. I'd tried to drop out of the election and failed—and now I was going to be secretary of the eighth grade! And all because of my friends helping me.

I started to laugh, and then Monique did, too. Harry let out a high-pitched giggle, then clamped his hands over his face, and that only made Monique and me laugh harder. We all just sat there laughing until we were doubled over, until people started to stare, until tears were streaming down our faces, and even then, we couldn't stop.

❧

Bella's ears pricked up, and a moment later, I heard the key turning in the lock. "She's home," I said, and Bella hopped off my bed and followed me downstairs.

In the kitchen, Mom was unpacking plastic takeout containers and placing them on the counter.

"What's for dinner?" I asked as the smell of curry floated into the air.

"I picked up some Thai food." Mom beamed at me as she shrugged off her coat and placed it on the hook near the door. Then she walked over to the sink to wash her hands. "Will you help me set the table, sweetie?"

"I—sure," I said, trying to act as if everything was normal as Mom hummed a little tune. "You're in a good mood." I wondered if it had anything to do with why she was late getting home.

"I am!" Mom pulled three plates from the cabinet. "I had a good meeting with someone at the college."

"What college? What meeting?"

Mom set the plates on the table and looked at me. "State. It was a meeting about their law program."

"What about it?"

"I'm thinking about going back to school. Maybe."

"What? Law school? Can we even afford that?"

"My work would pay for it."

"So you'd keep working *and* be in school?"

Walking over to the table, Mom pulled out a seat and gestured for me to sit down. Then she moved the chair beside it so that they were facing each other. When I took my seat, our knees were nearly touching. Mom reached for my hands. "Sweetheart," she said, "I want to talk to you about that meeting today."

"Mom, I'm sorry, I just—"

"No, no." She squeezed my hands. "It's okay. That meeting was great, actually, because it made me realize a few things. You know, I really can't bear to see you struggle or feel unhappy. It actually makes me feel sick."

"I know all about that, believe me."

"But that's my problem. I wanted to help you so badly that I just jumped in . . . and I didn't do the right thing."

"Bella is helping me, though, Mom."

Mom smiled softly. "She's a great dog, isn't she? But you're right—she's not ready to come with you to school. And that might not be the right answer, anyway. So I called Dr. Funk. She's going to meet with you once a week for the next few weeks, and then we'll see if she has any suggestions."

"I . . . That sounds great. I really like Dr. Funk."

"Oh, good. I think I'm just so used to helping Linden that I forgot how long it took me to learn what she needed in the first place."

"I knew you meant well . . ."

Mom petted Bella's head. "Thank you. But I just started thinking that maybe I've been worrying too much, too, and that's why I jumped in to try to fix things for you. Like, all of that advice about how you should try new activities and make new friends? Maybe I'm the one who needs to do something new. Like get my law degree. I'll reduce my hours at work and go to school part-time."

"You want to be a lawyer? But aren't you too . . ." I felt myself blush.

"Old?" Mom prompted. "Honey, I'm not planning to retire until I'm well over sixty-five. That means I've got twenty-five years. Once you girls are out of the house, what am I going to do with myself?"

"Well . . ." I blew out a huge breath. "I guess you're pretty good at arguing with people." I leaned forward to give her a hug. It was super awkward because our knees were in the way, but we managed it. The smell of her hair reminded me of all the times I'd come running to her when I was younger, and how she'd hold me on her lap. It felt like the safest place in the world. "You'll always be my wittle baby," Mom whispered. "And I'll help you in any way I can."

"Mo-o-om," I groaned . . . but I hadn't heard her nickname for me in a long time, and it actually felt pretty nice.

The side door burst open, revealing Dad, who beamed when he saw us. "Look who I found in the driveway," he said, stepping back so that Mimi could come inside.

I was still sitting close to Mom, so I heard her make a muffled grunt, but I don't think anyone else did. "Hello, Emilia," Mom said.

"Don't worry, I won't interrupt your cooking," Mimi said. "I just wanted to borrow that platter—oh! It looks like you're *not* cooking." She cast a disapproving look at the takeout containers. "Well, I guess that's how some people do it."

Mom's back was to Mimi, and I tried to keep my face neutral as she crossed her eyes at me, but I couldn't help it, I started to laugh. Then I tried to play if off as if I were choking. "I think I"—gasp—"swallowed a bug."

"Oh, you have bugs?" Mimi asked mildly. "I have some spray that's really effective."

Everyone was silent for a moment, trying to figure out how to change the subject. I figured I could do it.

"So!" I tried to make my voice as chipper as possible. "I have some good news!"

"Oh?" Mimi folded her jacket over the back of a chair and sat down expectantly.

"I won the election for class secretary!" I announced.

"Sweetie, that's wonderful!" Mom pulled me into another hug.

"You won what?" Dad asked.

"Class secretary," Mom repeated.

"I didn't even know you were running," Dad said. "That's great!" The corners of his eyes crinkled the way they do when he's really proud.

"Well, congratulations," Mimi put in. "Why didn't you run for class president?"

"I didn't want to run for class president," I told her.

Mimi shrugged. "I would like to think that by now

women and girls would want to be more than just secretaries."

"Oh, for heaven's sake, Emilia!" Mom brought her fist down on the table, and the plates rattled. "Do you think the Secretary of State is a secretary? Lizzie is happy! She won an election! She *won*!"

Mimi took a breath as if she wanted to say something, but Mom kept going. "And Linden is getting straight As!" Her voice went up an octave. "Straight As! Both girls are doing really well—there's no need to be so negative. Gah!" And then—I am not kidding—she picked up a fork and chucked it onto the floor, where it clattered and skittered until finally landing beneath the radiator.

Everyone just stared at that fork for, like, I don't know— it felt like forty-five years. Then my dad's eyes went to Mom. He looked shocked. So did Mom.

Finally, Mimi whined, "I was just trying to encourage Lizzie to be her best—"

Mom was about to reply when Dad cleared his throat and said, "Mother, that kind of encouragement isn't helpful." He put a hand on my mom's shoulder. "Francie has been working very hard to support the girls and get them settled. It's been a tough couple of years, but things are going well now. Okay?"

Dad was looking at Mimi, but Mom looked up at Dad with an expression that I hadn't seen on her face since . . . well, never. She looked surprised, pleased, and proud, and also like she might cry. She reached up for Dad's hand and he wrapped his fingers around hers.

"Oh," Mimi said. "Well, if you say so, dear."

"Let me get you the platter." In three steps, Dad was across the kitchen. He pulled the platter from the cabinet and thrust it into my grandmother's hands. Then he picked up her coat. "I'll walk you out to your car," he announced. Taking her by the elbow, he escorted her out the door.

Once the door clicked closed, Mom and I stared at each other. "I feel like maybe I started a chain reaction," I said.

Mom bent to pick up the fork. "I'm not complaining," she said. Then she tossed it across the kitchen, toward the sink, where it landed with a clatter.

"Three points," I told her.

She smiled. "Looks like we're all winning today," she said.

I leaned in and wrapped my arm around her waist. "I guess we are."

CHAPTER ELEVEN

Phobophobia—fear of phobias

I'm realizing that maybe this is part of what I've had all along. I'm not only afraid of everything—I'm just afraid of being afraid.

I've been thinking about what Ant said—how my brain is a powerful weapon. I had my first weekly meeting with Dr. Funk, and she said that if I can make up worst-case scenarios, maybe I can also make up best-case scenarios.

I think I'll try it.

"Where are you off to?" Dad asked as I shoved my feet into my sneakers. He was in his usual corner of the couch with his laptop balanced on his knees. Bella was curled up beside him, resting her head against his leg.

"Monique has a fencing meet," I said, bending down to tie my shoelaces. My rear pocket began to vibrate, and I pulled out my phone. "Hey, you," I said as Linden's face appeared on the screen.

"Lizzie! I can't believe I had to find out that you won the election from a random Picbomb post!"

"Oh!" I laughed. "Yeah! I was going to call you today."

"You could have sent a text." Linden looked hurt.

"You're always so busy."

Linden couldn't argue with that. "Well," she said at last, "congratulations! That's so great! And it sets you up really well to run when you're in high school!"

"Oh, ugh! I can't even think about that now. Hey, listen, can I call you later? I've got to leave for something."

"Call tonight," Linden said. "I'm not doing anything but studying."

"Bye, Linden!" Dad called from the couch. I flipped the phone around so that she could see him wave. "We miss you!"

"Love you, Dad. Is the dog on the couch with you? When did that start happening?"

Dad stroked Bella's head. Opening her eyes, she glanced up at him, then shut them again. "We hang out all day. She's my coworker."

"Only she's not very productive," Linden teased.

"Oh, she *is*," Dad insisted. "She's improving my productivity. Having a dog is very relaxing."

"Yeah," I said as I grabbed my jacket from the hook and crossed my eyes at Linden. "So I've heard."

It was only a ten-minute bike ride to the community center. The parking lot looked like a used car dealership specializing in family vehicles—minivans, SUVs, and station wagons had taken every available space.

Inside was a madhouse, with parents and siblings

clustered at food tables in the hallway. I made my way into the large auditorium, where people in white wearing mesh masks were attempting to poke one another, mostly without success. I could tell that none of them were Monique—her braids always give her away.

I was busy scanning the room for my friend when a voice near my ear said, "Hey."

Rex was standing beside me, smiling. He is a few inches taller than I am, so his face was tilted slightly toward mine. My heart gave a familiar stutter, but then seemed to remember itself and was functioning normally by the time I said, "Hi. What are you doing here?"

"Just . . . I have friends who do fencing." He gave a self-conscious shrug.

"Oh," I said. "Right."

"You here to cheer for Monique?" he asked. "That's cool—my friends never show up for my sports stuff." His eyes moved across the auditorium, and I followed his gaze to where Monique was seated on a bench. She hadn't spotted us. "You two are cool; I like your friendship."

Rex gave me a little wave and moved off in the opposite direction. "And hey"—he called over his shoulder—"congrats on winning the thing."

"Thanks," I said, but he didn't hear. As I walked across the auditorium, it occurred to me that I'd just had my first normal conversation with Rex. I hadn't stuttered or been weird at all. Huh.

"Hey," I said as I slid onto the bench behind Monique, who was engrossed in the match going on in front of her.

"Oh, hey!" she said, leaning backward so I could give her a little hug. "Oh no—ah!" She winced, reacting to the action in the match. A buzzer sounded, and Monique clapped. I guess someone won. Anyway, that seemed to release Monique from her spell, and she turned toward me fully. "Want to head outside?"

"You don't need to watch all the matches?"

"No, I'm good for about fifteen minutes."

Outside, the air was cold, and Monique sucked in a deep breath and gestured to her fencing outfit. "It was so hot in there! I hope you don't burn up—it's so sweet of you to come watch."

"That's what Rex said."

Monique's eyebrows went up.

"I just ran into him," I explained.

"Yeah . . . he's got friends on the team." She picked up the end of one of her braids, running it across her fingertips. "He's nice."

"Yeah, I know," I said. "He is. Listen, there's something I've been wanting to tell you. I saw you two hanging out at Yo-Ho."

Monique dropped her braid. "You never said."

"I know. It's hard for me to say stuff."

"Well . . . I asked him to meet me there because I wanted to make sure that he understood who was running for class secretary. I didn't want him to think it was a big joke."

These words landed on me like darts. *I could have known this days ago,* I realized. "Wow," I said. "That's . . . really cool of you, Monique. Thanks."

"No problem. He's easy to talk to."

"Yeah."

"What's that little smile? Stop smiling!" But she was smiling, too.

"No, it's—it's good, Monique. Like, I can tell he really likes you."

"We're just friends."

"Yeah, I get it. But . . . who knows, right?"

"Lizzie, you've had a crush on him for, like, a year—"

"But it didn't mean anything because I didn't even know him. Now I know him a little and he's nice and all, but—I don't know. My crush just kind of . . . dried up. We don't really have anything in common."

Monique looked doubtful. Then a thought seemed to occur to her. "Is there . . . do you have a crush on someone else?"

"What? *No.*"

She must have heard something in my voice because she cocked her head and said, "Really?"

"Well . . . maybe," I admitted. "I'm not sure yet."

"How interesting." She pursed her lips like she had suspicions.

"Monique!" Noah was waving frantically from the double doors. "Hey, we need you!"

My phone had begun to vibrate. I pulled it out as she hurried toward the door. "Coming?" she asked, turning back to face me.

"I'll be there in a sec," I told her. "I'm getting a call." I waved after her as she disappeared through the double doors, then tapped my phone. It was a moment before Ant's grinning face appeared. "What's up?" I asked. "I only have a minute."

"I want you to meet someone!" He disappeared for a beat, and I heard him say, "Come here, buddy." A moment later, a small blond Labrador appeared on-screen.

"Oh my gosh, who's that?"

"This is Melvin—my new dog!"

"Your parents finally said yes?"

"Finally, thanks to you."

"Aww." I felt myself blush. "So, uh. How old is he?"

"The shelter says he's three," Ant said. "He's really great—he can already sit and walk on a leash and everything. We'll have to get our dogs together and hang out!"

"Yeah!" I agreed. "Yeah—that sounds great."

"We can come over later?" Ant suggested. "Maybe around two?"

"Sounds perfect," I said. "But I've got to go—"

"I know, I know. Tell Monique good luck. I just wanted you to be the first person I told."

"I—" I was the first person he told? That was so sweet. Again, I wasn't sure what to say. "Okay, well, see you later, then."

As I slipped my phone back into my pocket, I took a deep breath. My heart was tap-dancing all over the place and my stomach felt jumpy. But not in a bad way. I didn't feel nauseous or scared.

Phobias? Not this time.

For now, it was easy to imagine a best-case scenario . . . one that didn't feel far-fetched at all.

Also by Lisa Papademetriou

Read on for a sneak peek!

DIY: How to Lose a Friendship
in Three Easy Steps

Last year was my first year of middle school. It was magical!

Just kidding.

It was actually a little rough, rougher than I thought it would be. Ward Middle School is okay. Everyone is divided into teams, and within each team, you have your own schedule. Confused yet? I was.

Anyway, my team last year was called the Meerkats.

My best friends from elementary school, Johanna and Avril, were on the Hurricanes. I didn't have any classes with Johanna or Avril. We just saw each other at lunch and when we walked to school and back home afterward. Which we did every day for the first two months of school, and then things got a little weird when the weather got colder and we were all doing different activities after school. But we still ate lunch together.

And then one day in February, I saw Johanna and Avril at lunch. I waved at them to come over, and Avril saw me, and then she pretended not to see me, and she walked right past me to get to another table. And Johanna followed.

I thought that was strange, so I brought it up when I saw Johanna after school. She said that Avril was mad about something I had said, so I called Avril that night. Avril said that she wasn't mad and acted like I was being supersensitive for bringing it up, so when we hung up I thought the whole thing was just a massive misunderstanding.

The day after that was the 100th day of school, and I had filled two jars with one hundred M&M'S each and I made two cards listing a hundred things that were great about Johanna and Avril. It was no big deal, mostly just inside jokes. I slipped the cards through the vents in their lockers and I had the M&M'S hidden in my lunch bag. I was sitting at our usual table and waiting when they walked into the cafeteria. I waved, but Avril blew right past me. Johanna gave me a little *I'm sorry* look, but she went with Avril. Neither one of them said anything about the cards.

I sat there, all alone, for what seemed like forever. Tears made everything blur, and my throat was tight. Finally, I went to a bathroom stall to cry, but the tears wouldn't fall. It just felt as if my whole head was encased in stone.

When I got home, I ate all two hundred M&M'S, not bothering to call either one of my supposedly best friends. I knew they would just lie to me and tell me it was all in my imagination.

We didn't sit together at lunch for the rest of the year.

Johanna lived down the street, so she couldn't avoid me completely. But whenever she talked to me, she acted like she was doing something wrong or breaking some kind of rule.

Still, I kind of thought that, well, maybe they would get

over it. Like, our friendship switched off so suddenly . . . maybe it could switch on again.

Look, I know that there are bigger problems in the world than this. But all I can say is that when you've been friends with someone for years and then all of a sudden you're walking to school and home by yourself, it feels . . . bad.

Oh, sure—people always say make new friends, like it's that easy. I don't think I have to tell you that there is a huge difference between a friend you have had for six weeks and a friend you have had for six years. Huge. I had other friends, but they were, like, not my good friends. You can't be good friends with just anybody. It isn't easy to find someone who really gets you.

Do you know what the worst part is? It's all those songs and T-shirts and stupid TV shows that sing Friendship Is Forever and all that junk. Because I really believed it; I really thought Johanna and I would be friends forever. Avril? Not so much. I really only got to know her in fifth grade. But Johanna and I had been friends since we were little. There's still a part of me that thinks we can make up. Maybe.

So that's my other project for seventh grade: Make up with Johanna.

Or make friends with someone who gets me.

Or both.

ALSO BY LISA PAPADEMETRIOU